INTRUDERS FROM THE STARS

By
ROSS ROCKLYNNE

I0541396

ARMCHAIR FICTION
PO Box 4369, Medford, Oregon   97501-0168

*For more information about Armchair Books and products, visit our
website at…*

www.armchairfiction.com

Or email us at…

armchairfiction@yahoo.com

EARTH IN THE GRIP OF AN ALIEN BEAUTY

Earth lay helpless and supine before Bess-Istra—a lovely but malevolent woman from beyond the stars. Yet how was this possible? She possessed only a single spaceship and a small force of soldiers. But her weapons were like nothing mankind had ever seen. She could ravage the planet's surface in a few short days—and there was no way the combined forces of man could possibly stop her. The Earth was completely vulnerable to her unrelenting lust for conquest.

Only a New York reporter and a Christian missionary from the wilds of Africa had any chance of swaying her intentions. And that chance seemed hopelessly slim—especially since she had captured the hearts of both men.

FOR A COMPLETE SECOND NOVEL, TURN TO PAGE 119

CAST OF CHARACTERS

BESS-ISTRA
She was stunningly beautiful, but was she the savior of a planet, or a bloodthirsty tyrant from the depths of outer space?

BILL VAN ASTOR-SMYTHE
An old fashioned cracker-jack reporter, only this time his scoops weren't confined to the inhabitants of Earth!

JOHN STEVENS
He served God with a faith as strong as anyone's, but could this faith withstand the allure of a devastating alien beauty.

BANDRO
As head of the International Police. he was put into a position of extremely high power—perhaps too much power.

SAB-HALLO
His brilliant but twisted scientific mind had created the kinds of weapons only dreamed of in man's worst nightmares.

THOMAS REYNOLDS
Surrounded by great men, all he wanted to do was go back to his home in the jungle—but it got him more than he bargained for.

PROLOGUE

IN A planet that is far from Earth—how far away we dare not guess—the wooden slopes of the Valley of Kopeljin were alive with the dreadful sounds and radiances of battle. Dreadful to her who, at the rear of her armies, sought only, in her great, consuming rage, to save face, to avenge the ignominy done by those who had brought about her downfall.

But:

"Retreat!" she screamed. "Men! Why do you tarry when your mistress needs you? Retreat to the Knob, for this is the end of our empire!"

The end of empire indeed. Oh, the long, glorious months when Bess-Istra, the lowly, spat-upon slave-girl, sat on the throne of the planet, held its peoples in thrall!

Oh, the long, glorious reign that was ended when the prime minister, who sat at her right hand, turned against her, betrayed her, harried her, hurled her own armies against her, drove her back inch by inch, until she stood here with her dying loyalists around her, with their blood staining her arms and face.

The end of empire!

The tears of a scalding rage furrowed the grime of her face. The remnants of her legions were beating their way up through the wooded slopes of the Valley of Kopeljin— beating their way up and dying without grandeur as the limitless forces of the enemy hurled balls of green acid fire into their hopelessly depleted ranks; dying, as explosive lead pellets monotonously, chatteringly issued from the high chalk cliff to the right; dying, as enemy pilots, stretched out on their tiny, down-swooping gliders, vengefully dropped pill-size pellets from the night-darkened sky; dying as the pale, colorless, fan-shaped radiance of a monstrous beam fluffed across the width of the valley, fatally touching only those who did not carry the protecting *bik*—touching them and shriveling them slowly to nothingness; dying—but with the name of Bess-Istra on their lips!

Bess-Istra! She had flared for one moment, like a swift-dying nova. But the people of this planet would not soon forget her, would long remember her after she was gone, and their remembrances would be the remembrances of—*fear!*

She choked back her rage, her grief, to fondle that thought. She had left her imprint—aye. And now she would go...

"Retreat!" she screamed down into the bowl-shaped depression where the last of her men held a feeble line. "To the Knob. All is over! Bess-Istra commands you to follow after her, to guard her, to escort her to the Citadel where she shall make her escape!"

Most came, scrambling up the hill toward her; a few remained behind with a cannon-ray projector, to guard the retreat. Bess-Istra would never see them again, nor they her. But they were content, for to a man they worshipped her, looked upon her very footprints as hallowed ground, though she had plunged a planet into rivers of blood, out of her own selfish passions.

Her chief officer moved behind her with long, gaunt strides as she swiftly followed a precipitous path. Before her, two soldiers hacked away the obtruding branches of the waxy trees, so that her way might be without hindrance or discomfort. And so they finally came to the base of the Knob, the great, immeasurably thick dome of natural iron ore which capped this hill, and whose interior formed—the Citadel.

BESS-ISTRA stopped, her breasts heaving. She made a motion to her chief officer.

"The valve, Bandro. Quick…"

Bandro stepped forward on the moist, leafy ground, his long slim fingers sweeping camouflaging weeds from the broad, man-size valve that would give entrance to the Citadel. While he worked at the complex lock with sure, delicate touch, his impassive, gray-seeming face turned toward Bess-Istra.

"We could yet make a truce, Mistress Bess; by that path at least we would retain life. By the other, we invite death."

She struck him across the face—savagely.

"You dare suggest it!" she cried. "You, Bandro, whom I trust. You would have me humble myself to him who deceived me? Let me not hear of this again."

Bandro stood rock still, gray eyes lidded and concealing his emotions and his thoughts; his love for this girl at that moment turning into hate.

He turned woodenly back to the valve, worked on it for precious moments. Bess-Istra faced affrightedly into the backward distance, hearing the dreadful sounds of an annihilating battle, knowing that her thousands of remaining men were shriveling away under the awful weapons being turned against them.

"Quick! Oh, quick!"

"The valve opens, my lady," said Bandro.

And indeed it did, just as the pale ray across the valley began to walk across the ground toward Bess-Istra and the hundred loyalists who surrounded her. They had no protection against that ray, they had no *biks*. But once they were in the Citadel, there were few man-made forces that could rout them out or harm them within the space of several days. And by that time, Bess-Istra and those of her empire who loved her would be gone.

Bandro now led the way down through the palely lighted corridor. One of Bess-Istra's lieutenants stood at the mouth of the tunnel, gathering in the remnants of the army, screaming at them above the furious cacophonies of battle. The valve would remain open as long as there was the mere chance of rescuing one of Bess-Istra's men. Then it would be closed—and though the might of the enemy was hurled against it, they would not destroy that impregnable door. The only way they could get through would be to utterly wreck and annihilate the Knob itself; then it would be too late.

They came into the great central room of the Citadel without fanfare. One of Bess-Istra's mechanics came quietly to her.

"You have need of the ship, then, Mistress Bess?"

"Our very lives depend on it now. And the ship is prepared for its long journey into the depths of space?"

"Another day will see us prepared."

"Good. It shall be a day of rest. I am weary of death, and my men are weary also," she turned to Bandro, who stood to her right, regarding her impassively from his darkly mottled eyes; stood with his billowing cape tossed loosely over his arm, the blood-red scimitar, symbol of Bess-Istra's short-lived reign, on his swelling, powerful chest. But impassive though he was she sensed his deep hostility.

Her glorious, scarlet lips curled now. "I know your thoughts," she whispered. "You think that I have but dragged you with me into a death-trap. You curse the day your lot was ever cast with mine."

EMOTION at last touched his gray skin, quivered the nostrils of his straight nose. His voice quivered also, but so deeply that one could almost count the separate vibrations.

"I gave up life and love and family that I might at last taste power—that I might feel in me the strength of millions of men as they did my will."

He sucked a lip-shivering breath through his teeth; his chest rose and fell quickly. He ground out, speaking under only the greatest restraint, "And now what have I? What? A rat-hole to dwell in for awhile, while the enemy pounds from outside—and a spaceship to be dumped into, to be gassed, to sleep for uncounted years—and not even to know on what barren celestial flotsam I shall crash to my end, along with her who is responsible for my fate."

"You presume…" she cried, white with fury. Her hand dropped to the deadly spastic-gun at her curving hip. "Mark you, Bandro, I would as lief kill you as not—"

"As you have killed others for as little reason," Bandro shot out. The wild expression of utter panic now crossed his face like wildfire. "A truce!" he suddenly cried, so that dozens of those near heard him. "A truce I Demand of Bess-Istra that she makes a truce with the enemy. Aye, and for what reason does she not? Because she knows that, though we who have supported her would be given leniency, *she* would die.

"But she is sending us into certain death. This dream of hers—this fantastic belief of hers that the escape ship will hurl through space for countless years, and land on a planet of her choosing—land *safely!* Will hurl through space, to land while we are lying in frozen sleep, unconscious of elapsed time. It is a mad dream, this plan of hers—"

Bandro never knew what hit him. He stiffened, stood stick-like for one shocked second. Then he knotted up, head between his legs, teeter-tottered a moment, then rolled to his side, where he lay quiet and unconscious, the muscles of his body straining to contract in unrelenting spasm.

Bess-Istra straightened from her savagely tigerish half-crouch. She sheathed the spastic-gun, in which tiny lights were dying. She laughed a harsh, unpleasant laugh.

"Fool…" she spat. She stepped forward, kicked the helpless man. Then she whirled, stood fork-legged, glaring at the dozen men who looked at her with sullen faces. She said no word, but held their eyes until the flush of shame stained their brows.

Bess-Istra laughed again. "And you are fools, too, for listening to Bandro's indictment and considering it. Know you not that I would not betray you?"

Under the bewitching angry languor of her glorious eyes they could not long maintain their sullenness. Their faces dropped. And Bess-Istra cried, "About your business then, soldiers! There is much loading of armament into the hulls of the escape ship to be done; armaments and munitions that will give us fair start in the conquest of another planet not far from here. Begone—and take this upstart Bandro with you and roll him into an empty corner of the ship. He is still a valuable man, and he will be grateful to me for taking him with me when we awake from our sleep."

So saying, Bess-Istra walked with supple, yet fatigued, stride to her quarters; but her brows were drawn down frowningly, sadly, over her barbarian eyes. An episode was drawing to a close, a golden day had turned to lead; she wanted but one thing, now, wanted it passionately—the neck of the man who had betrayed her between her fingers…

ONE day passed; one day being that length of time required for that far-distant planet to turn once on its axis.

The enemy harried the Citadel with the full outpouring of their frightful weapons. And finally, a bare few moments from the time that the great, armed escape ship was to be plummeted into the deeps of space, Bess-Istra was called to the television cubby, where the hard, yet war-weary, eyes of her arch-enemy bit into hers.

"I call you," he said wearily, "only because I have the good of my people in mind, Bess-Istra."

She interrupted him. "Traitor! Beast whom I trusted. Would that I could but drive a dirk into your heart..." She made a savage, utterly unrestrained motion, came close to the television screen until it seemed that her blazing eyes would sear him. "Do not talk to me of the good of your people. Such words are but hypocritical mouthings. You seek the good of the people no more than did I—you seek only to flaunt your own power over them, for you yourself have felt the acid of lowly, ignominious beginnings."

"Not true, Bess-Istra," he made sad answer, and on his weary face there was pity for her. "I have never been driven by selfish motives."

"What do you want of me, traitor?"

"Of you, Bess-Istra, I want only yourself. For all your tyranny, the tyranny that at last compelled me to betray you, the people could be swayed by you as by no other in all our history. They loved you, though you whipped them."

A muscle in his hard, drawn face twitched. There was pleading in his eyes. Unconsciously, he extended his hands in a pleading gesture.

"Forget this mad desire for power, Mistress Bess. Remember only of the great good you can do the people. This cruelty that you have so often shown is but an outward garment in which you clothe yourself. The cruel avenging, tyrannical Bess-Istra is not the true Bess-Istra. The true Bess-Istra is gentle, soft, merciful, feminine—a woman both lovable and admirable. Bess-Istra—return to my side and rule with me."

11

Her lashes lowered over her glorious, gold-flecked eyes, her full lips writhed into a taunting yet voluptuous smile. "You love me, fool," she said huskily.

His shoulders fell. "Yes. But it is not for that reason alone that I wish you to return. It is because I know there is in you more good than evil. Bess-Istra—together we could rebuild a war-shattered world. Will you return?"

FOR a long moment she said nothing, savoring the hope that grew in his eyes with every moment of her hesitation. Then she burst into a wild, taunting laugh. *"No!* That is my answer, my final answer," she cried, "and I am glad that you asked me—glad that you love me—for now your torture at my refusal will be all the greater. Now, take your face from my sight forever!"

The muscles of his face slowly whitened. He said in a horrible voice, "I am compelled to slay you and all those in your garrison, Bess-Istra."

Her hands were on her hips, her eyes widened in mock amazement. "Indeed...know then, that when you destroy the Knob, and break into the Citadel, no soldier, and no Bess-Istra shall be found. The Citadel shall be an empty shell for no life shall be here."

He studied her with pain-shadowed eyes. His voice was flat.

"How?"

And she laughed again. *"How?* Now let that mystery torture you to the end of your days. Farewell!"

His face faded as she flipped the toggle switch—faded forever. And on Bess-Istra's face was only a look of gloating triumph. She could leave this planet now, knowing that in great measure she had avenged herself on the man who had caused her downfall.

She thought over what he had said concerning her softness, her inner gentleness. A dark sneer grew on her lips. The utter fool for thinking such obvious nonsense!

She sought out her chief mechanic. "Tell me, now. Is the ship ready for its long journey? Have the soldiers been loaded into their acceleration chambers? Does the ship bristle with those very weapons which harried us into our hole?"

"All ready and waiting your command, Mistress Bess."

She laughed joyously. "Then let us leave this planet forever. Relieve Bandro of his spastic slumbers, bind him in the acceleration chamber which his rank affords him; for if he were to undergo the Sleep with common soldiers, they would have no respect for him and so would be useless to me. Inform him that I forgive his loss of control—inform him that I graciously retain him as my second in command.

"Come now; there is no reason to tarry longer. To the ship…"

Nor was there reason to tarry longer. The giant cylindrical ship was loaded with its thousand remaining soldiers of the army; with deadly weapons; with armaments and munitions. And its nose was shoved into the tube-runway that would give it exit from the Citadel—and from the planet.

Empire's end! But so certain was Bess-Istra that there was no fatal flaw in her fantastic plan, that she knew another empire, perhaps greater, lay beyond the vast sweeps of space the escape ship would take her. Another empire! A new empire for Bess-Istra, once the spat-upon slave-girl.

And so an era ended, the era of Bess-Istra upon that planet. Nevermore would she be seen there—nevermore. She was gone, gone so swiftly that no eye knew of her going—for the escape ship snapped away into open space much as a watermelon seed is flicked away when pressed between thumb and index finger.

Flicked away—immediately soared into tremendous, appalling speed—left that solar system under the guiding hand of the navigator—plunged headlong into the unimaginable emptiness of interstellar space—settled down to a steady, void-consuming pace—a pace it would continue, according to Bess-Istra's plan, for thirteen full years.

THE navigator, the brilliant scientist who had invented the first spaceship under the guidance of Bess-Istra, swung around on his chair, his too-bright eyes fixed on hers.

"It is done, Mistress Bess," he breathed. "My genius has succeeded in the most monumental calculation ever undertaken by mind of man. Though the next solar system lies a full light-year distant, though the planet which you and I have studied in detail through the *tele*-eye travels on a complex orbit, the escape ship shall land there gently, safely, thirteen years from now. And we shall conquer that planet, vanquish its peoples…"

"Then," said Bess-Istra, "then we are ready for—the Sleep. Oh, Sab-Hallo, you have done well indeed, and shall have a position of power under me. But tell me, Sab-Hallo. By what means shall the ship land with no hand to guide it?"

"You need not worry, Mistress Bess. Long before the ship lands, radio-echoes will let robot controls know how far away the planet is. The ship will brake its speed accordingly. And when the distance from the planet is zero, the ship's speed relative to the planet will be zero.

"Other instruments that measure the heat given off by those people we intend to conquer will make certain that the ship lands on an isolated spot.

"And as soon as the ship lands, a strategically placed lever will activate a mechanism that will dissipate the Sleep-gas, will provide normal air. Then we shall awaken, in full possession of our senses, ready to do battle."

Bess-Istra, in spite of herself, felt an inward shrinking sensation. Here in the control room, nothing but a transparent partition staved off vacuous space. Stars—stars in endless number, lonely, lonely. How deep space was; how bottomless and frightening.

"And," she whispered, "what if we should perchance miss our destined landing place, Sab-Hallo? Would we…die?"

"Die?" The thought was terrifying to the scientifically conceited Sab-Hallo. "No—*no*. I have made provisions. The Sleep-gas will last—forever. And some day the ship would land on another habitable planet, perhaps even in another solar system."

"It is good," she sighed. "But of course, we will land on the planet of our choosing, and to think otherwise is foolish. Come, Sab-Hallo, leave the controls—and let us pump the ship full of the Sleep-gas…"

And it was done. Soldiers drew the straps around themselves in response to the command that was issued. They breathed deep of the odorless vapor that soon filtered in from the ventilation ducts; breathed deep and slept.

Bandro, thoughts alive with his hatred of Bess-Istra, slept.

And Sab-Hallo, unafraid, pleased with himself, certain of the perfect operation of the many strange instruments that composed the ship, slept.

And Bess-Istra lay languidly on her couch in the observation room, her glorious, gold-flecked eyes surveying empty space. Soft, gentle, transparent straps held her to the couch, for there was no gravity.

There she lay, breathing deeply, no longer afraid of the star-dusted void, but rather admiring its chilling beauty. It was necessary that she should lie here in full view of that abyss. Necessary to abate the sense of loneliness, of wretched depression that now gripped her. There was something soothing, comforting in that velvet darkness…

As soothing as the vapors that now were drawn into her lungs, and that now stole from every tiniest cell of her body any semblance of life; caused her lungs to cease breathing, her heart to stop her blood to halt in its veins and arteries; her brain to stop thinking. This was—the Sleep.

And Bess-Istra—*slept!*

SLEPT for how long? Who knows? *Not* for thirteen years, as she and Sab-Hallo had supposed. For the escape ship did not land on the planet at which it was aimed!

Did *not!* The scientists of that planet were wiser than Sab-Hallo had known. Wiser by infinitely more than most of the many races of the universe that bear the human form. And more peace loving. Those scientists had their own *tele*-eye, and with it they searched Bess-Istra's ship; searched it, knew its history, its terrible purpose—understood all this when the ship was a mere hundred million miles away.

And so from that planet that Bess-Istra thought to have conquered came a powerful beam of force which gently, unjarringly, grasped the escape ship; changed its course, ever so subtly; shunted it into a new path but slightly different from the old; guided it out of that solar system; sent it boring without change of speed out into interstellar space again. That planet would never be bothered by Bess-Istra.

And that path the ship took and kept—and would keep until, perchance, it should enter another solar system far removed from this one.

Then would it land automatically on another planet?

Who knew? Certainly not Bess-Istra, who slept with her lifeless face to the changing star...

And how long ago was this? When did all this happen?

Longer ago than any of us dares to think...

CHAPTER ONE
"They Worship Another God!"

CRACK! *Crack!* Crack!

"Hey!"

The ejaculation was a roar of rage that shivered the dripping lianas snaking through the wet foliage of a mid-summer African jungle.

"Put down that rifle! Quit shooting at me! I'm no damned Japanese soldier!"

"Sorry, brother," an austere voice at last spoke from behind the banana plant. The gun was lowered. "The very lions of the jungles these days might be Japanese—who, I agree with you, are damned; damned, almost to the point where they are beyond redemption. However, had I hit you, you need not have been alarmed. The Lord giveth, and the Lord taketh away."

"Praise the Lord," gasped the thoroughly unnerved voice of Bill van Astor-Smythe, ace legman of the New York Corey Features Syndicate, "and *spare* the ammunition…"

He broke from his shelter in the ravine, his feet sinking ankle deep in the decaying humus of the Portuguese East African jungle. His black hair was in disarray, his khaki shorts and shirt torn and befouled with swamp mud and studded with tenacious burrs. Bloody thorn scratches made tic-tac-toe patterns on arms and thighs. To his bosom, as if it were purest gold, he clasped a portable typewriter, which—upon examination—would have proved to be vintage 1929. No matter. It worked and *any* typewriter that was available and that worked was a precious thing indeed in this year of 1944.

As he weaved across the clearing, he was grinning a cockeyed grin in spite of the evidence that an unfriendly jungle had mauled him around.

"Hip, hip, Reverend!" he yelped. "As I live and breathe, I'm glad to see a human being again. The incident is forgiven and forgotten. Which way to the mission and a juicy alligator steak? Boy—what wouldn't I give for a hot bath Astor-Smythe style."

He tottered suddenly. He sat down on his portable typewriter, propping his dizzy head in his palms.

"Wow...who'd have ever guessed those Japs would come along and riddle those poor British lads? Didn't have a chance, not one of them. I was in the rear of the British column and we were just an hour out from Lorenzo Marques when they ambushed us. Bet you anything I was the only one who got off with a whole skin... Damn...this is fierce!"

He had a pounding headache, nausea. He couldn't see straight. But suddenly the man who had shot at him was holding out a canteen and a quinine pill. Bill washed the pill down gratefully. After a few more dizzy moments he jumped up and weaved a circle around his typewriter.

"Boy! Hell...that's better. Fever's gone, but my head is ringing. Thanks."

The kneeling man rose. He was dressed in shorts, too, but a ministerial closed collar was around his neck.

"Thank the Lord, brother; I'm but His servant." he intoned.

"Thank God, then. I'm a servant, too. I serve the press, a sort of god in its own right. Let me introduce myself, Reverend—you are a reverend of course?"

"As the Lord maketh me, so am I."

"Okay, okay. But what's the handle?"

THE other's brows drew down over studious, serious eyes that couldn't have seen more years than Bill's twenty-six.

"Handle?" His lips broke into a puzzled, almost shy smile. He said softly. "Oh...I am the Reverend John Stevens—and this—"

He pointed to a nondescript, pinched-looking companion who now emerged from the jungle and stood near him.

"—and this is my assistant, Thomas Reynolds."

Bill shook Reynolds' hand.

"Pleased to meet you, Reynolds. And you, Johnny...er...Reverend," he also grabbed at Stevens' hand, but dropped it hastily when he saw Stevens wince. "And I'm Bill van Astor-Smythe, of the snooty, snobby, nasty, nose-raising, blue-blooded van Astor-Smythes. Ain't—I mean isn't that something to live down? You should have seen the old man when I shipped myself off to England three years ago as a special war correspondent-on-trial for my syndicate."

The memory made him shout with joy, so that a half-dozen polychromatic parrots ceased their painful jargon and fluffed their wings with frightened squawks.

The Reverend John Stevens had cause for alarm, too. He closed his hand around Bill's arm and looked around affrightedly.

"Please, I beg you..."

"Eh?"

"Japanese! I have no way of knowing what inroads they have made into Mozambique, nor where the British front is laid down. But such an untoward sound as you have just made might draw them in this direction if a party of them were near."

"Yeah, yeah. Sorry. I see what you mean. Maybe we better get back to the mission, huh? You *have* got a mission, haven't you?"

"By the grace of God, yes. It's a little place, but I'm able to say that the several hundred Bantus who live in this region have been converted to the true religion. That is—"

He paused. His eyes shifted worriedly, as if he were conscious of a sin he had committed. A sudden despair tugged at his lips. "That is, I believed until yesterday that they had been converted. Now it seems...doubtful. Yesterday morning, a great many candleholders and candles were missing from the altar. I questioned my houseboy patiently and...and he broke down. He gave me no details, but I understand that my parishioners are—" he dropped his eyes hopelessly, "—well that they are worshipping another god of their own choosing."

"You don't say. The dirty—"

"Oh, please don't condemn them, for they know not what they do. But...well, I am not on my way to the mission as you suppose, but to the village where I understand the new idol has been erected."

He patted the Garand rifle that had given Bill van Astor-Smythe an uncomfortable few minutes. His lips, which had seemed pleasant only, and a little shy, now turned hard.

"And then I shall strike down the clay image that my straying sheep have raised in mockery of the true God," he raised his hand high, and his blue eyes acquired an expression of terrible wrath. "The Lord our God," he cried, "is exceeding fearful when wickedness tarries in the breast, my children; he shall flay from thee the sins which I, and my father before me, have sought out and tried to destroy, verily—"

"Cut!" Bill van Astor-Smythe yelled.

He was standing with his hands on his hips and grinning. As Stevens lowered his hand and blinked at him, Bill grinned. "That kind of junk is for the movies, pal. It's sob-sister stuff, see?"

"Sob-sister?" Stevens blinked. Then he got a woe-begone expression on his face, and all the religious rapture faded. His shoulders slumped. "I understand," he said unhappily. "The mission has been my home all my life, you see, and during the last five years—since my father died—" He stopped, gulping.

Bill looked at him with pity. "Sure, sure, I get it. You've been cooped up here away from the world all your life, playing spiritual nursemaid to a bunch of frizzy-headed Zulus. Well, pal, it looks like the end is in sight. Day after tomorrow, the Japanese army will be pad-padding through your jungle and making a GHQ out of your mosquito-proof parlor, Johnny."

STEVENS' dismay showed in his eyes. "Oh…not really…" he pleaded. "You mean that Mozambique will fall to the enemy? You mean to say the gallant British won't hold their own?"

"I double-mean it." As carelessly as Bill spoke, his fists knotted, and sparks of anger showed in his narrowed eyes. "And not only that, Madagascar across Mozambique Channel is filthy all the way to the interior with Japanese battalions. It's the pay-off, the big blow-up—and the Allies are in a he— that is, a melluva hess."

Bill picked up his portable. "Come on. I'll help you play truant officer on the hooky players having truck with the old-time religion. Better give me another of those quinine pills, though. Da—darn! Wish I had a *kepi* to shunt this water down my back instead of my neck."

Bill was feeling a thousand times better as they forced their way through the dripping tropical forest. He was light of heart, cocky of tongue, and breezy of manner under normal conditions, and normal conditions for him were very close to a state of affairs that would madden most other people. Bill had sat on the chalk cliffs of Dover with a telescope and his typewriter, as the hundreds of fishing smacks came beating across the Channel from Dunkirk loaded with their grimy soldiers. On the way from Bataan to Corregidor his typewriter keys had given the Japanese shore batteries some tough competition—at least from the standpoint of racket. And by plane to Australia he kept up the infernal noise. Only, the New York Corey Features Syndicate did not consider his cabled news infernal. That syndicate smeared Bill's reportorial adventures all over the bottom of the front page of ninety daily newspapers throughout the land.

And from Australia to the Solomons, to the Aleutians; a stretch on Midway; some madness on the Libyan Desert, bouncing along in a tough American jeep hot on the heels of Rommel's African army; and from thence across the Mediterranean where the Allies were striking at Italy, the "soft belly of the Axis dragon."

Then new developments. The Suez-Red Sea route to the South Pacific was not yet safe for Allied shipping, and supply ships were making the long journey down around the tip of Africa—the Cape of Good Hope. Thence these supply ships were constrained to beat up along the East Coast, passing directly through Mozambique Channel, which was flanked on one side by Mozambique (Portuguese East Africa) and on the other by the island of Madagascar.

In Mozambique Channel, Axis submarines had sunk tons upon tons of Allied shipping, using Madagascar as a secret base. To prevent the Germans from taking over Madagascar from the neutral French, and thus controlling the sea route entirely, Britain had taken over the Island in 1942.

But Madagascar was only half the problem. Across the channel was Mozambique, which might at any time be seized from neutral Portugal by Germany, and which already harbored a Nazi consul who used his diplomatic immunity to cable Germany fatal information concerning Allied ship movements through the Channel.

Britain had completed the job by gaining Portugal's tacit assent to occupy Mozambique, also. They held the Portuguese possession for hardly more than a month when the Japanese launched a simultaneous attack on both island and mainland.

And now, in midsummer of 1944, the Allied sea route around Africa was imperiled.

BILL VAN ASTOR-SMYTHE cheerfully explained all this to the Reverend John Stevens and his companion. Neither having been isolated, was apparently well informed.

Stevens was leading the way, seeking out paths and shortcuts around and across swamps thick with mangroves.

"A boy scout, too..." Bill gasped admiringly. "You find your way around like a bush native, Johnny. Someday I'll do the same for you, maybe, along the complicated wilderness trails of li'l ol' New York. If the enemy doesn't don't get us—which they probably will."

Stevens said nothing; he kept on pushing ahead, his jaw righteously grim. Bill felt a flash of respect for the young missionary. Even though the Japanese were bound to make things uncomfortable in a few short days, Stevens was going to disabuse his "parishioners" of the notion that there would be more than one true God.

Bill for the first time seriously considered this alleged new god. He was curious. What or who were the natives worshipping? Probably nothing very exciting, of course. Probably nothing at all. Stevens had merely heard a rumor, which was just that—a rumor and nothing more. But still, perhaps Bill could get a story out of it. A half-dozen sticks of type, maybe...

And so he was shocked when, with the gloom of falling night, they came to the edge of a glade and saw that which threw all of Bill's (and, indeed, all of humanity's) smug beliefs in the uniqueness of the planet Earth into a cocked hat.

A spaceship!

CHAPTER TWO
The Awakening

THE three men suddenly stopped in the concealing growth of wild maize on the edge of the oval-shaped glade. Stevens' breath drew through his teeth. His arm shot out and forced his two companions to their knees.

Bill gaped. Slow dizzy thoughts began to parade across his consciousness. The scene at which he looked was beyond the pale of common sense.

Hardly twenty feet away from him, seated cross-legged on the ground, were a half-dozen white-haired, fuzzy-headed Kaffirs. They were sitting in front of drums, which were made by stretching antelope skins across hollowed-out tree trunks. The Kaffirs were moaning softly, weirdly, almost inaudibly. They swayed back and forth, while their fingers brushed at their drums and made a wild barbaric rhythm which Bill had to strain his ears to hear.

Their heads were raised toward the "god" they were keeping vigil over—a sleeping girl!

The girl was not all. There was the cylindrical-shaped ship. At least, Bill had the crazy feeling that it had to be a ship. It had numerous square portholes, and long, fin-like appendages towards one end. But if it was a ship, it was no ordinary ship, for its incredibly hard-looking golden surface had a slight tinge of greenness, like the patina that covers ancient things. And though this patina was not extremely noticeable, Bill had the feeling that this ship was older than any man-made thing. *Perhaps older than man himself!*

All this Bill took in with a mere glance. But the greater part of his attention was captured by the girl. His breath caught in his throat; there was in him an emotion that was like pain. He was lost in her compelling, other world beauty. She lay motionless, head resting on the glossy black pillow of her hair, a coverlet barely concealing the perfection of her body. Her eyes were closed. Her cheeks were tinged with the flush of life, her lips were scarlet as blood, set into a piquant, child-unhappy expression. But her breasts did not rise and fall. She might have been but a painting. She might have been merely a corpse—if Bill had not known instinctively that she was alive.

"No wonder," Bill heard himself saying in a low, crazily-wavering voice, "no wonder they think she's a goddess. Oh, Lord…I could worship her myself."

"You do well to pray to your Lord," the Reverend John Stevens whispered, in acid *sotto voce*, "if such are your thoughts! What wickedness swells here? Who is this shameless creature? What is her purpose in stealing my converts?"

Bill felt a flash of irritation. "Boy…you sure take yourself seriously, don't you, Reverend? Shut *up!*"

Stevens' mouth opened and closed. He blinked and gulped. Reynolds, his assistant, said uncertainly, "See here, now—"

"See here—nothing!" Bill shunted himself a step closer to them, whispering fiercely. All his flippancy, his cocky acceptance of a dangerous situation, was gone. In its place was the deadly seriousness of a tough, quick-thinking reporter who sees a story beside which all other news stories pale to nothing.

"This is something that is bigger than you or me, Reverend Reynolds. And why? Because that girl is not a native of the planet Earth…"

"Not…not a native of…the planet Earth?" Stevens repeated the words in a tone of horror. Then his face grew very stern indeed. He leaped to his feet with a cry of anger. "Blasphemy!" he cried. "Impossible! My father taught me that God created Heaven and Earth and populated Earth with creatures made in his own image. Other planets are therefore lifeless, and the Lord did not intend man to travel between them."

THEN he apparently regretted his temper. The flame in his eyes died down. But he said sternly, "Do not interfere with my duty as a minister of the Gospel."

And he whirled, and with long, plunging stride broke into the glade and confronted the drummers.

Bill van Astor-Smythe stood up, his hands on his hips in disgust. Talk about your fire-breathing sky pilots. Here was one in the flesh. The drummers had leaped to their feet, gesticulating, jabbering wildly in the Kaffir tongue. But the Reverend John Stevens talked back at them, even more bombastically, and suddenly they began to cower, and then fell to their knees, their heads lowered. Bill heard them mumble meaningly, "OurfatherwhoartinHeaven—"

They went through the whole Lord's Prayer, and then, with wails of terror, ran into the jungle, apparently back toward their village. These oldsters were, Bill guessed, chosen solely to keep watch over the villagers' new object of worship when the tribal ceremonies did not include her.

"They realize their sin," Stevens said triumphantly. "Please come out, Mr. Astor-Smythe; Mr. Reynolds."

It was with a strange sense of eeriness that Bill stood in front of the spaceship, for such he knew it to be. The glorious creature who lay on a couch in what must have been the observation booth the ship was utterly oblivious of events—had been oblivious for how long? Bill shivered. The thick, glass-like material which sealed the girl in was scarred with long, white, gouged streaks, straight as a ruler—as if, perhaps, meteors moving at incredible speed had struck glancing blows, had left their marks. Inside, on the glass plate, were star-shaped hasps or locks, which might have accommodated keys.

The girl was fairly visible, partly because of brightening moonlight, partly because of the rows of lighted candles in their candlesticks which had been placed on the ledge beneath the transparent partition beyond which she slept. Nonetheless, Stevens drew his flashlight and spotlighted her upper body and head.

Stevens' voice was gloomy when he spoke. "A creature of evil and wickedness, verily; a temptress who, if she should wake, would be more dangerous than a serpent of the jungle."

Bill grinned. "Don't stare so hard at the young lady while she's in bed. It's unethical. Besides that, it just ain't right."

Thomas Reynolds flushed scarlet. His mouth fell in his confusion. "I was only trying—" he began in protest.

"We were trying to determine whether the—the creature really came from another planet," Stevens hastened to his aid. Stevens' own boyish cheeks were red.

Bill chuckled. "Save it, pals. I know what you were trying to determine—whether you'd have what it takes when she does wake. But never mind about cogitating too hard about whether she really came from another planet. Take one look at the ten-legged spider dozing in that web spun on the outside of the glass there. Hey—there's a whole half-dozen of them!"

IT WAS true. The spiders, if spiders they could be called, had woven their strands across the glass-like material, anchoring them in the sharp corners where the glass-like material melted in the hard metal of the ship. But they were *ten-legged* spiders!

"See what I mean?" Bill demanded tensely. "You won't find any ten-legged spiders on Earth. Spiders are *arachnida;* they have eight legs by definition. That probably proves this ship came from another planet. These eggs may have gotten caught in the corners of this window, somehow endured the cold of space, and then hatched when the sun struck them."

The beam Stevens held on the girl shook, as if the entire philosophy of his life was being rearranged. He desperately tried to grab at a straw. "That—that spider up there has eight le—" He stopped, biting at his lips when the "spider," as if in answer to the challenge, moved in its web, and stretched out two additional legs which had been hidden beneath its body. He faltered, unable longer to question the argument.

Bill took the facetiousness from his voice. "Play the beam around the other parts of the ship, Reverend—hold it! There…"

A vast excitement rippled through Bill's breast. Suddenly he had dropped to one knee, dropping his portable.

"Look at this!" he yelped. "A lever of some kind! And if it isn't the lever that will wake up this girl and—or maybe open up the ship—"

"How do you know?" the missionary asked sharply. He and Reynolds had similarly dropped to their knees. In spite of themselves, they had been infected by Bill's excitement over a chance discovery.

"I *don't* know."

Bill wrapped both hands around the foot-long bar of metal that protruded from the base of the ship—the only such protuberance to be seen anywhere.

"But I'm almost certain of it," Bill continued vibrantly. "Look here…this isn't a lever so much as a plunger. It was designed to be pushed upward. When the ship landed, it would force this plunger upward. But the ship, by pure chance, rested its aft section on the limb of that fallen *baobab* tree there. The plunger was prevented from touching solid ground. It obviously didn't fulfill its function when the ship landed."

The Reverend John Stevens flicked the beam over the plunger. He said slowly, "And perhaps it was a good thing it didn't, Mr. Astor-Smythe. I have a conviction about that girl in there and it is not a pleasant conviction—*don't...do...that!*"

"It's already done," Bill said in satisfaction. It had required no more than a steady upward pressure to slide the plunger out of sight into the belly of the ship.

Bill glanced sidewise at Stevens, grinning. He enjoyed the look of stricken uneasiness on the young missionary's face. Stevens, strangely, had an almost *religious* fear of the sleeping girl. How silly that was! Showed what happened to you when you were isolated from the rest of the world and had nothing but a Bible and a flock of Zulus to keep you company—

And it was at that moment that Bill heard the hissing sound... At that moment he sensed terrible danger!

HIS eyes popped. Coming from invisible apertures in the hull of the ship he saw sudden streams of a yellowish vapor. He caught a whiff of it. It spread mortal terror through his soul as his brain went suddenly dizzy.

He leaped to his feet and back. He caught chaotic glimpses of Stevens and of his assistant, Reynolds. They had seen the gas too. Not only seen it, but—breathed it! They were tottering, staggering away from the ship, or trying to stagger away. But suddenly they fell on the ground.

Bill himself fell, futile, scalding curses leaping through his remaining thoughts. Stevens had been right. There was something hellish about this whole thing, about this ship, about this girl. Why had he ever had the bad sense to push that plunger up? It had obviously released a gas designed to slay any life near the ship! For Bill knew he was dying as he fell.

But as he fell, he saw the glorious sleeping creature stir— saw her limbs move in life—saw her lips part—saw her eyes open with awareness of an external world. He had been right. The plunger had been designed to wake her—and perhaps others of her kind within the ship. He groaned in abject horror of what he had done, and felt life slip away...

CHAPTER THREE
Peace for the Planet Earth!

WHEN Bill van Astor-Smythe regained consciousness he knew with certainty that he was the captive of the people from the stars. He already was quite certain that the sleeping girl was not the only inhabitant of the ship. She would not have come alone.

Even as he lay there, his mind struggling out of its torpor, his bones like lead, he was reasoning his way out of confusion. Where had this ship come from? Why? Bill shuddered; for some reason he felt that if he had only listened to the Reverend John Stevens, he could have averted a terrible catastrophe, which still lay in the future.

He did not regain full consciousness immediately. But for a lucid second, as through a blur, he saw three figures standing over him. Two were men, dressed in alien clothes. The third was the ravishingly beautiful sleeper who no longer slept. They were wearing strange helmets that looked like those used in football. Bill knew that such a helmet was on his own head, and on those of Stevens and Reynolds who lay on the floor of the room with him.

Between the helmets ran wires.

That Bill saw before he lost consciousness again. But he felt strange forces plucking at his brain...he felt his thoughts running with incredible swiftness over every memory of his life, and every forgotten memory, as if somebody were turning the phonograph of his mind at incredible speed.

Then he was awake—and being hauled to his feet!

"Men of the planet Earth." an alien human holding a strange weapon snapped. "You will fall in between us. Mistress Bess will speak to you…"

Along with the dazed Reynolds and Stevens, Bill fell into line between two guards dressed in resplendent metal-braid uniforms. They were marched down an echoing corridor. They turned left into a lavishly draped room. And here sat Mistress Bess—the Sleeper!

Bill felt the same painful lump in his throat. She was so beautiful. Beautiful beyond the laws of nature.

They were brought to a standstill.

Studying them closely, the girl leaned forward, her brief silken costume spangled with diadem jewels that clustered in her hair like bright galaxies strewn on ebon space.

"Leave me, guards." she spoke suddenly. "I do not require protection from those who are my friends." Her hand came down as the guards bowed themselves out.

Mistress Bess smiled—smiled a voluptuous smile that was as kindly as it was subtly taunting. And suddenly, for no good reason, that smile enraged Bill.

His square jaw came out. "Friends? Like fun!" He snapped the words insultingly, his fists knotting. "If you call gassing us a friendly act, think again. Or maybe that's your idea of how to say 'hello, how are you' on your planet?"

He sneered.

Her eyes, gold-flecked, turned cold. She half rose on her chair. Then she sank back, apparently restraining herself.

"You speak rashly, handsome one," she spoke softly. But there was the sharpness of a razor beneath her voice. "But no matter. I am glad you have already ascertained that we have come from another planet. That is true. You must also realize that the gas that stole your consciousness was released entirely automatically, was designed only to protect us from hostile creatures when the ship landed, to awaken me and my officers and my thousand soldiers from their long, long sleep."

"Soldiers?" Stevens was breathing hard. "And why do you bring soldiers to the planet of the Lord? Nay, do not answer. Already, the Lord my God has spoken the truth unto me." His arms flung up, and his voice was terrible as he fearlessly stepped toward the Mistress Bess.

He cried, "You are a scientific race, versed in the arts of the destruction of lives and property—*and you have come here to conquer the planet Earth...*"

THE cry rang through the gorgeously tapestried room, and for a moment it seemed to turn everybody into statues. Then Bill yelped in hopeless disgust, "Oh, *nuts!* Come back here, you dam—you blankety fool!"

He stepped forward, grabbed the African sky pilot's arm, and pulled him back. He turned to Mistress Bess.

"Sorry, Mistress Bess. He—ah—he knows not what he does—oh, hell, he's got me doing it, too. I mean, he's got a fantastic streak a mile wide—and not a magazine stand within three hundred miles. I don't think you're any angel and I don't feel as if you're my bosom friend, see? But I've got sense enough to know that nobody's going to try to conquer any planet with an army of a thousand men and only one measly ship. Sorry he blew up."

Her eyes were narrowed, and Bill thought he saw the trace of an ironic smile. He frowned—but at that moment the door opened. Into the room stepped the two men whom Bill vaguely remembered having seen just before he regained complete consciousness.

The taller of the two broke into a rapid, harsh flow of language. Mistress Bess spoke sharply.

"Speak in English, Bandro. These are...our friends."

The crescent eyebrows of Bandro shot up. There was a demoralized expression about his mouth. It was evident that some discovery had shocked him.

The smaller, stockier man at his side broke into less excited speech. "It is of no great importance Mistress Bess," he snapped. "Bandro is unduly alarmed, even though we entirely missed the planet for which we started—"

"What?" The girl cried the word out in shocked unbelief. "But...but you yourself told me that there were no other solar systems within many light-years—hundreds, perhaps. That...that means that we have slept for—" dread drew the rosiness away from her cheeks. "—*for how long?*"

The other's voice was somber. "Longer than we dare to think, my lady. But what matter? To us it was but the fraction of a moment. We closed our eyes and opened them as the plunger dissipated the gases in the ship. And the ship fulfilled its purpose. It has landed us, safely, on a planet populated by beings of our own calibre—beings whom we can—"

"Stop!" She cut him off. She was breathing heavily, her face ghastly. "No matter. It is as you say. We must thank our gods for guiding us to safety on a livable planet—"

"There is only one true God! You foul creatures of the devil—"

"Shut *up!*" Bill swung Stevens around again, his eyes blazing. "Get hold of yourself, you—"

"I cannot stand by and see my religion blasphemed," Stevens cried excitedly. "This—"

Bess-Istra leaped to her feet. "Stop!" she cried sharply. "Will you have us throw you in chains, fool? I am not of a mind to tarry when there is work to be done—when there is a great need to be met..."

SUDDENLY a soft slyness tugged at her lips. She left the dais on which she sat, her bare, golden legs moving with silken stride. She stopped a few feet removed from the three men. Reynolds, who had been standing a little behind his superior, had been staring with hypnotic fascination at Bess-Istra from the moment they had come into the room. Bill felt much the same, only worse. There was something about this girl that rang warning gongs in his brain, but at the same time she made him experience an emotion that was overwhelming—and frightening.

She said huskily to the Reverend John Stevens, "You wrong us when you infer that we could intend the conquest of your planet—a planet where a God named the Lord rules. No! Our purpose is different—our purpose is kindly."

"What—" The man named Bandro spoke sharply, but cut himself off, his mottled dark eyes suddenly lidding.

"Yes..." spoke Bess-Istra. Her breath came more quickly. "You know, men of the planet Earth, that we are now speaking your language. Does this seem like magic to you? It is not. By means of an instrument which we, in our language, call the *vothet,* but which is a great deal like the hypno-bioscope invented years ago by one of your countrymen, we were able to transfer from your subconscious minds much detailed information."

Bill remembered the helmets. "Yes," he nodded. "You learned the language that way, then?"

"Learned," she said, "not only the language, but also much about the planet Earth. For instance the nations of your planet are at war, are they not?"

Bill's mind was brought back suddenly to a remembrance of the conscienceless hordes of Nazis and Japanese who were bringing misery and ghastly destruction to the world.

She added softly, "And the Allied nations of your world have their backs to the wall, are fighting a hopeless battle, are they not? In the Pacific the Japanese are throttling you. In Italy, the Nazis are about to trap Allied armies. Your cause is well nigh lost. In another few months, the democratic nations of the world will be at the mercy of beasts. Is it not true?"

And Bill knew it was true. Few men dared to believe that it was true. They fought on, refusing to believe they were already doomed. But this girl, from out of the depths of space, could look at the whole picture without prejudice. She knew. And she—

He drew his breath in suddenly. A startled thought swept across his mind.

"You mean—?" he cried.

"Yes…" The glorious face of Bess-Istra seemed transfigured with an inner glow.

"Men of Earth," she cried, her voice a clarion peal, *"we who have come from space are going to stop the war and spread peace and contentment throughout the world…"*

CHAPTER FOUR
"—Beleaguered Isle of Madagascar!"

TO STOP the war! The thought seized at the innermost cells of Bill's brain. He grew dizzy with it.

He was not a sentimental sort of person. He had deliberately hardened himself to witnessing misery and death in their worst forms. The possibility that these mysterious people from the stars, with their super-science, could bring to an end the conflict scouring the world free of every decent human thought, awoke in him a choking hope.

Did she mean it? Could she mean it? Or were her words a mockery? Was she truly the devilish creature that the young missionary thought she was? That Bill thought she was? No! To have the hope withdrawn would be too much to bear.

Bill swiftly looked at the other occupants of the room. He whom Bess-Istra called Bandro stood fork-legged, face impassive, but with his eyes hinting his secret thoughts. Near him stood the shorter, stockier being with the glittering eyes; he was looking at Bess-Istra, lips curled in a vain, meaningless smirk. The Reverend John Stevens' jaw was hanging; but it was Stevens who broke the pulsing silence.

The zeal of his religion was in his eyes. Somehow he was standing straighter, somehow his eyes were flashing with a godly fire. But this time, Bill was thankful to see, no austerely dogmatic cry erupted from his throat. Instead, there a humble dignity to his words.

"Mistress Bess," he said humbly, "if I have offended you with my suspicions, I pray your indulgence. But I was wrong—wrong! I had thought you to be the devil's own, but this offer of yours, to free the world from a desperate, horrible tyranny—well, the thought can have originated in none but a good and true mind. I—"

Her gold-flecked eyes were gazing at him oddly. "Good and true?" Her eyes brooded, narrowed, as if she were struggling with a thought that stunned her.

"Yes, yes…for after all, and I quote: 'He who loveth not his brother whom he hath seen, how can he love his God whom he hath not seen?' Mistress Bess, we are all children of God, though we worship him under other names; and so now, if your intentions are indeed what you say, I throw open my heart to you, I give you my love—"

"Ixnay on the ovelay," Bill van Astor-Smythe sang out. He was grinning. "Cut it out, parson. What he means, Mistress Bess, is that your offer to save the world for Roosevelt and Churchill rings the bell with all of us—and how."

His excitement overrode any restraint he might have had in the presence of a beautiful girl.

"You mean you actually could do it? Slap down the ears of those dirty minions? Drive Hitler and his bunch back to the last front?"

BESS-ISTRA still looked at Stevens, at his boyish, radiant face, his eager blue eyes; still looked at him, as if his words lingered in her mind. Then she returned her attention to Bill. She studied him. She began to smile. She threw an amused look at Bandro and the other.

"Speak to him, Sab-Hallo. Tell him of what we could do."

The stocky, broad shouldered man known as Sab-Hallo smirked. He addressed Bill, his glittering, self-pleased eyes holding Bill's as if in contempt.

"The *vothet,* the machine which taught us your language and something of your world, gave us a general picture of the war that is being waged on this planet. It is a devastating war, of course, but nothing to what we on our planet—"

"Sab-Hallo…" Bess-Istra spoke.

He bit at his tongue and cringed a little. He said humbly, "I was merely about to remark that on our planet, although we excelled in the arts of peace, our science was such that we had great and marvelous weapons stored away in secret places. These weapons we have brought with us in our epochal flight across the void. They are weapons besides which your artillery and bullet-throwing guns are as nothing; your airplanes, your battleships, your tanks, your deadliest gases and bombs—these are children's toys. On this impervious, practically indestructible ship which I, Sab-Hallo, have constructed, we have weapons which can level whole armies."

"Yes." Bess-Istra took up the tale smoothly. "As we shall level and destroy the armies of those who menace the freedom of your world—"

"No!" Stevens cried the single denial, pleading in his voice. His arms extended. "Mistress Bess, we must not. If we are going to bring salvation to the world, can we not do it peacefully, bloodlessly? For if we bring the peace we cannot do it through hate. Justice is the Lord's."

"Hold everything," Bill interposed swiftly. "Back down, Johnny. You don't look gift horses in the mouth—"

And Bess-Istra interrupted him, her eyes wide on Stevens and his outstretched hands. "Stay!" she commanded. She spoke musingly, "Yes, it can be done. Why—why, a bloodless victory…" The thought seemed to stun her.

He who was known as Bandro strode forward, his heavy metal-braid sleeves slapping against his smoothly muscled arms.

"But…but, Mistress Bess—" he burst out in what seemed like anger. "This has never been your manner—"

She faced him. Her lip curled. "Quiet, Bandro," she exclaimed softly. She smiled, tawnily, voluptuously. "After all," she said in a softer, more yielding tone, "are not these our friends? Do we not desire to please them?"

For a long moment he returned her gaze. Then his anger dissipated and he strode woodenly back to his place.

"Very well," he spoke at last, into the silence that settled. His lips curled into a peculiarly crooked smile that made Bill shiver. "Do as you wish, my lady," he murmured, and there was a slight sarcastic tone to the words. "You have ever chosen to amuse yourself by strange means."

SHE whirled toward him, and the double-lensed pistol at her side was in her hand and directed toward him. "Mark you, Bandro!" she cried in a tone of rage. "Once before you stood against me—but I reinstated you, made you my second in command; forgave you. But your insolence cannot longer be brooked. Will you stand in the way of this great mission which I seek to undertake for the…the good of our fellow men?"

Bandro stood still, faint contempt in his eyes.

She sheathed her weapon with a sliding clatter. "See to it then."

Abruptly, all passion was gone from her face. Bill made a mental note that here was a girl who might appreciate a good punch to the jaw at the opportune moment. Damned if he'd ever let her pull a gun on him. But in the meantime it might be more to the point to play along with her.

He kept his thoughts to himself, as Bess-Istra turned to him, her full scarlet lips pursed with what Bill knew was deliberate coquetry. Knowing it didn't seem to be any antidote. His heart beat painfully. And she must have guessed the emotions in his breast, for a half-taunting light grew in her glorious eyes.

He said huskily, with just the shade of counteracting insolence that was necessary to set her back a trifle on her heels, "Okay, Bess. Where do we go from here? We've got a world to save. And every minute we stand here making small talk, somebody dies that shouldn't have to."

Her mouth tightened imperceptibly, but she immediately regained her balance.

"We begin where you, Bill van Astor-Smythe, say," she said coolly. "The *vothet*, as you may guess, is not powerful enough to cause all the information we drew from your brains to be impressed on our brains. The complete picture of world events is not before us. But you, being a—a reporter? —you would know of such things. Command me then, O Bill. To which battlefront shall we proceed—and shall we destroy, or merely render our enemy helpless?"

The Reverend John Stevens' eyes were shining with a godly joy. He grasped Bill's arm.

"Brother," he cried, "good tidings at last sweep across the world. Peace and good will toward men is at last to be a reality. Praise the Lord. And may I make a suggestion?"

Bill was faced with a staggering decision. Where to start on this impossibly monumental task? "Go ahead," he invited dazedly.

"As a trial action," Stevens said glowingly, "why not save Madagascar and Mozambique from the damned Japanese?"

The idea caught in Bill's brain like tinder. He snapped his fingers. "Swell!" he cried. He whirled on the voicelessly watching girl, paying no attention to the ironic mirth in her barbaric, gold-flecked eyes; nor to the enigmatic half-smiles of Sab-Hallo and Bandro. He began to talk in rapid staccato fashion, outlining the plan that had come to him.

Across Bess-Istra's face flashed respect. "You would make a good strategist on my own planet," she murmured speculatively.

"You had wars on your own planet then?" Bill demanded, eyelids flicking upward, in the beginnings of startlement.

She momentarily seemed to bite at her lip. She said easily, "No...No, of course not. Many thousands of years ago there were terrible wars. But in the era in which I lived all was peace and prosperity, and men loved each other."

SHE flirted a casual look at Stevens. Stevens was so excited, Bill thought, that he would very likely blow a cylinder if some steam wasn't let off. This was his dish. An angel had come from Heaven who sorrowed for the woes of men and was magically empowered to put a stop to it.

Bill felt a faint thrust of alarm, momentarily. Something— what was it?—didn't seem quite right. Oh, nuts—his touch of malaria was making him nervous.

Bess-Istra now turned with a silky motion toward Sab-Hallo.

"The ship is ready to lift off; all my soldiers are awake and have eaten. They are ready to stand at their posts to receive orders to operate their weapons should we have need of them."

"All can be made ready within a few of those Earth units of time called the minute," Sab-Hallo replied, "but the only weapons we will need to accomplish our task are those I shall operate from the control room. Mistress Bess."

"Good!" Bess-Istra drew a sharp breath. Her eyes sparkled with an excitement that had suddenly drenched the very air. "Are we ready? Then to the control room, Sab-Hallo. Lift the ship out over the great sea that Bill says is to the east—and find the Japanese supply fleet, which is at this moment sailing with munitions and reinforcements toward the beleaguered isle of Madagascar..."

CHAPTER FIVE
Soft Belly of the Axis Dragon

"THERE it is!" Bill was sitting in an acceleration chair, part of a semicircle of people who leaned backward and looked up at a broad white view-screen, which showed a perfect picture of the cobalt, white-capped ocean spread out below.

The ship, a mere thirty minutes ago, had leaped up into the sky with a tremendous burst of speed. And there was no acceleration! One hardly knew one was moving, for the acceleration chairs created an etheric field that robbed each atom of an accelerating body of its inertia.

Seated in the semi-circle were Bess-Istra, Bandro, the Reverend John Stevens, and Bill van Astor-Smythe.

Thomas Reynolds had pleaded of his superior to be allowed to go back to the mission. He was a simple soul, and confessed that these strangely alien people frightened him. Stevens was glad to let him go, for the mission needed someone to tend it. Reynolds left the ship before it left the ground.

Bill was pointing to a fan-shaped area of white-caps now. It was miles below, but it was certainly the wake churned up by the Japanese fleet.

The spaceship plunged down out of the stratosphere toward its goal. Excitement plucked at Bill's nerves, sent the blood singing through his veins. Could these people actually do what they claimed to do? It seemed impossible.

He glanced sidewise at Bess-Istra. Her scarlet lips were parted with the same excitement Bill felt. She was watching the growing fleet with interest. Bill saw clumsy cargo ships with deep wells and thick funnels. There must have been a dozen of them, loaded with packing cases that were filled with enough munitions to keep the Japanese on Madagascar and Mozambique going; would keep them supplied until the Allies surrendered.

The ships were closely bunched. Except for two destroyers they were traveling without convoy.

But as the spaceship dropped toward the fleet, there were signs of action. Sailors on deck went mad. And suddenly from each of the ships came flashes of fire and an appalling racket like continuous summer thunder. They were firing two-inch shells!

At the same time, the convoying destroyers stepped up their paces a notch, and from their funnels poured thick streams of smoke. At the same time the destroyers erupted with anti-aircraft fire.

Bill winced, knowing that no ship could stand up under that withering fire. But Sab-Hallo suddenly burst into a titter of delight.

"Pitiful…" he cried. "They think to harm my wonderful ship—seek to harm the ship which even fierce-driven meteors could not damage. The fools—the useless fools. Mistress Bess, say the word, and I shall show them the might of our planet—shall utterly destroy and sink their fleet with one blow."

She bent on him a cold, withering glance. "Do so and it will be your lot to join them. Render them helpless and drifting—it is all I require."

Bandro now turned in his chair with the motion of a panther. He spoke in a low fierce tone, the dark furrows of a vast impatience over his brow. "Why should we spare them,

Mistress Bess? They are troublemakers. They and their nation must be completely negated before our—before the plan can succeed! Before the peace can be consummated. Was it ever your manner—"

"It is my manner *now,*" She spoke slowly, as if puzzling over something. Then she shrugged. She smiled a hard, peculiar smile and snapped at Sab-Hallo, "Drop closer. Spew their ships from stem to sterns with the golden disks. At once, for there are things to do and this is a larger world even than that one from which we came."

"It is good, my lady," muttered Sab-Hallo, sullenly.

His deft long fingers touched at a control sequence on the console board and Bill saw a beautiful sight...

GOLDEN disks, thousands of them, spinning rapidly, fell from the belly of the spaceship, swiftly approached the cargo ship directly beneath them. Bill heard the missionary give a cry or unbelief as the golden disks spun through the decks and disappeared; touched at the chattering guns and seemed to be sucked into the metal of the guns.

And those chattering machine guns, which threw two-inch shells with incredible rapidity, ceased their fire—*jammed!* And at the same time acquired a brilliant golden glow.

And then the cargo ship, a swarm with panic-stricken Japanese, began to lose headway. Smoke ceased to pour from its funnels. It lost speed.

But by that time, the spaceship had darted toward another Japanese craft, straight into its futile anti-aircraft fire. Again the golden disks spun rapidly downward—and again! Within five minutes after the spaceship had attacked, the Japanese weapons were entirely silenced, and the whole fleet was an aimless flotilla of flotsam.

A fleet unable to move under its own power.

"And Madagascar is two hundred miles away!" cried Stevens, pounding his fist exultantly, yet softly, restrainedly, on the arm of his acceleration chair. "Oh, this is indeed a great day for man!"

"But—but how did it work?" Bill cried, amazed. "Bess—Mistress Bess or whatever—"

She shrugged carelessly. "It was nothing. The golden disks were but magnetic force fields, which had an affinity for metal. They act as staples that bind the moving parts of a machine together so tightly that no force can sunder them. The Japanese fleet will float helplessly until after we have made the peace."

"And when the Japanese discover that those men and supplies they needed aren't coming through they'll know they can't keep on fighting," Bill said joyously. "They'll retrench, try to consolidate their gains. The British will follow them up and hack them to pieces. *Wow...*"

He suddenly let out a yell that made Bandro leap to his feet with a curse that turned Stevens' face red, even though the curse was made in another tongue.

"Where's my typewriter? *I've got a deadline to meet!*"

Deadline!

And Bill van Astor-Smythe, legman extraordinary for the New York Corey Features Syndicate, made that deadline—and a hundred more infinitely more important.

Scoop after scoop! Scoops for which any journalist would give thirty of the ripest years of his life.

Bess-Istra, the glorious mystery girl from the stars, had smiled with indulgent patience at Bill that day after he yelled for his typewriter.

"Of course," she said smoothly. "You will want to let your people know what is happening. So be it. Bandro, lead our great friend Bill to a room where he can be uninterrupted."

AS BILL went away with Bandro, Stevens was talking with Bess-Istra, quoting eager reams of Biblical quotations, his face on fire. And Bess-Istra was listening with complete attention, an odd, thoughtful expression in her eyes.

Bandro turned with his hand on the knob of the door of the room to which he had brought Bill. A curious malevolence was naked on his face.

"I wish to give you a warning, friend Bill," he said when he had Bill's attention. "Do not look with too bold an eye on her who is known as Bess-Istra!"

Bill put his hands on his hips. "Hands off, eh?" he snapped. "Says who? You haven't got a lease on the pretty maiden, have you?"

Bandro took three quick steps toward him, nostrils flaring. "Fool!" he sneered. "You will be caught in her toils like numberless others. Don't you know that she is not what she seems?"

"Don't you know that it isn't any of your business whether I do or don't know? And quit talking behind a lady's back..."

They glared at each other.

Bill spoke again, levelly, harshly, "Let's you and me get off on the right foot, Bandro. I don't like you. I never will like you. Get it?"

Bandro was voiceless. His gray skin grew dark. He at last said in a strangled voice.

"We will remember that, friend Bill."

He turned and was gone. Bill wrinkled his nose and said, "Nuts."

Within less than a minute, he was attacking his typewriter in a very frenzy of creation.

He was halfway through his story when Bess-Istra entered the room. Bill ripped a sheet from his typewriter in a daze. He rose awkwardly, face flushed.

"Forgive me, my friend Bill," she said smoothly; "but I have gone to the trouble to make your story credible to the outside world. Are you yet finished with it?"

"A half-hour yet," Bill said dazedly. Then his eyes sharpened. He said slowly, "Yes…yes, of course, I will have trouble making my editor believe. But how have you—?"

"Finish your story," she cried. There was a warm, almost childish delight in her voice. "And then I will show you!"

Bill finished his story, but curiosity was rife in him. He read over the typewritten pages, and a huge grin of satisfaction spread over his face, which was beginning to acquire a reddish growth of beard.

"Boy…" He whispered to himself, lovingly stuffing the manuscript into one of the legal-size envelopes he kept with his typewriter. "Hot stuff!"

He looked up at Bess-Istra, wandering through the gleaming, instrument-studded interior of the great ship. She led him to an alcove where Stevens, Bandro, and Sab-Hallo were standing. Nearby, next to a slanting board with red buttons, a metal-braid clad soldier stood. Bess-Istra motioned to him.

He pressed a stud—and the entire side of the alcove fell away, letting in the daylight of the outside world; and as the gangplank touched and was still, Bill cried out in unbelief.

The ship had landed on the roof of the New York Corey Features Syndicate Building!

BILL knew that was so because, two blocks away was the Empire State Building. Bill had often seen that gigantic structure from this roof.

But mostly he knew it because a half-hundred of the employees of the New York Corey Features Syndicate had surrounded the ship, yelling and running, and waving their hands excitedly.

Stevens' eyes were bulging. "New York City!" he gasped. He almost looked frightened. He had never seen any city bigger than Mozambique or Lorenzo Marques.

"By...the unholy...hinges of...Hell..." Bill said, spacing the syllables out. "What the—" But he got the idea. Nobody could fail to believe this story now—particularly with his editor standing in the forefront of the crowd over there, jaw hanging slack.

Bill burst into an excited roar.

"Mac!" he yelled. *"Mac!"*

He raced from the gangplank onto the roof; he grabbed the dazed man's hand, shouting senseless things. Then he thrust the manuscript into his hand.

"Print this! Spread it over the front page of every newspaper that wants to pay a fancy price for a first-hand account of the saving of the world! I'll give you a story a day from now on, until it's over over there. And my percentage jumps from 60% to 80%! Okay?"

"Okay..." gasped the startled editor. "But—but what—that is—Bill—" He floundered.

"Save it!" Bill laughed joyously.

"You'll get the whole story from that manuscript. Goo'bye!"

He turned, sped into the interior of the ship, and the gangplank soughed into place behind him. And a few seconds later the ship from the stars hurled into the air toward "the soft belly of the Axis dragon"—toward Italy!

For Bill had decided that there lay the next logical striking point against the monstrous forces that were throttling the world...

CHAPTER SIX
Victory on the Second Front

BESS-ISTRA stood close to Bill. He could feel her bare arm on his as they looked into the view-plate. He wondered if she were doing it intentionally. It was doing things to his insides.

"There's Italy," he exclaimed. "The real European Second Front. It was preceded by the battle for Tunisia. When the Allies won that, they had the whole coast of North Africa for a jumping-off place to attack Hitler; for North Africa was, in effect, an airplane carrier…a *big* one."

Bandro stroked at his sharp-pointed chin. The ship was dropping slowly downward and forward, following the low mountain range that girds the west coast of the Roman boot.

"And the war strategy of the Allies—of your inadequately armed American forces?"

"They may have been inadequately armed from the standpoint of what you think is adequate," Bill retorted, disliking the insolence that Bandro at times deliberately put into his tones, "but from our standpoint we had the goods. *Had* it! But now the Americans and the English, three hundred thousand of them, are about to enter another Dunkirk…"

His face was pale with agony as he said it. He hadn't realized until he had listened to a newscast, which Bess-Istra had picked up for him, that the Allies were facing such a black future in Europe. Now they were dying like flies.

"As for their strategy, they hammered Italy from Africa with hundreds of big bombers, destroying port after port. But the Italian navy, commanded and manned by Germans, escaped and is loose in the Mediterranean. That navy played hell when we ferried men across the sea from Tunis to Italy. But the British navy chased them, and halfway up the coast of Italy, where the mountain range breaks, we landed our armies. For awhile it seemed like things were going good, but Hitler meanwhile was bringing in reinforcements from the Russian front and the Vichy French forces were drafted, too.

"The Allies, in the first week of fighting, completely drove across the middle of Italy to the Ionian Sea, cutting off all communications in the boot part of Italy. But in the next three months the Nazis proved too much for them. As things stand now the hard-fought for position in Italy will be entirely lost."

"The inhumanity of man to man," said Stevens hopelessly. "And after the war, what plan of action will keep down the beast in man—keep it down forever?"

Sab-Hallo laughed a high-pitched laugh and rubbed his hands together. His eyes were gloating. "We shall solve that problem, too," he said throatily. "There are few problems that my genius cannot solve. "For instance, I have a—"

"Quiet..." Bess-Istra snapped. "Your genius will earn you an early death if you do not remember that I command you in all things."

"Very well, my lady," the squat, broad-shouldered scientist said sullenly. But Bill, watching him, saw a grim look pass between him and the perpetually sneering Bandro.

BESS-ISTRA gripped Bill's arm. Bill found himself looking deep into her barbaric eyes. And he knew they were barbaric. He knew that she was willful, strong of mind, ready to temper, thoroughly spoiled—dangerous, maybe. And yet his attraction for her, deadly though it was, was growing, no matter how hard he fought it. And he knew that she knew it—for now there as a taunting mockery in the impertinent curl of her full red lips.

"And now," she said in a breathy manner, "if we render the enemy army helpless, if we entirely destroy resistance; the Allies will be able to gain control of all Italy, will be able to depose this large-jawed man called Mussolini."

"And not only that," Bill said vibrantly, "but our armies will be ready to pour into Germany. For Hitler will simply be unprepared for this blow. He won't be able to muster his forces."

"So be it," she spoke coolly, and turned to Sab-Hallo. "When the mountains break, turn eastward until we come to the front where these gallant Allies are dying. We shall destroy all resistance with the gas-ray."

The ship hurled into a sudden speed and the sky over the postcard-pretty Mediterranean, blurred. And when the ship stopped, they were looking down at the battle—a battle that made Bill's blood run cold. He knew that never before had man seen such horror. Never had so many and such murderous weapons of artillery been gathered in one place; nor so many tanks; nor, if it were known, had men fought with such ferocity.

Although in this part of the world it was early afternoon, the only light was that furnished by frantic search-beams stabbing the sky for dive-planes; by cannon—mostly 155-mm howitzers, Bill guessed, supported by 75s and 100's—which belched fire that was purplish-red like the blood of reptiles; by tracer-bullets leaping across devastated open spaces from hidden pill-boxes where machine-guns chattered.

No light, except from these weapons. For a black pall of smoke lingered from horizon to horizon.

But in that light, Bill saw great tanks spitting out their death at retreating Allied soldiers. Saw heaps of bodies bloodying that never-to-be-forgotten battlefield.

And then, as the ship from the stars hovered, he saw field artillery turned upward!

Bill was aghast. "Those damned Nazis are firing at us!" he cried wildly. "They'll bring us down before we can accomplish our purpose…"

And indeed, little puffs of light were exploding about and near the ship.

"No." Stevens was pale. He stammered, without conviction, "No…the Lord is just. Though we walk in the valley of the shadow of death, he will not permit us to die when our mission is so great."

"That God whom you call the Lord," said Bess-Istra, and Bill for the life of him could not tell whether she was being serious or faintly sarcastic, "must indeed be powerful. For this ship is impervious to ordinary missiles such as those. Indeed, only the green ray of death and disintegration could harm it. Still," she added, apparently in deepest thought, "it does not seem probable that your God the Lord would have had the foresight to have created this ship solely for the purpose of defeating your enemies."

The Reverend John Stevens said seriously, solemnly, "But it may well be the case, Mistress Bess. He works in strange ways his wonders to perform."

There was an ironic, retrospective smile to her lips, and her eyes wandered, as if they were gazing backward along the trail of memory. "Strange," she muttered, and her voice was curiously metallic. "A strange god indeed that does not bid its worshippers to strive arrogantly and impetuously, cruelly, for power. In my province, where I was born, there was a god who— But this is foolishness. Sab-Hallo, on this Axis army that seems likely to defeat our friends the Allies, you will use the gas-ray. And use it until all their legions have fallen in stupid slumber, easy prey for the embattled Tommies and Yanks!"

THE gas-ray. In the next two hours, the two natives of the embattled planet Earth saw that alien weapon used with awful effect. Sab-Hallo touched a stud on the edge of the instrument panel. And Bill saw a soft, yellow-spangled cone of light flick downward toward an anti-aircraft battery that was pouring a solid stream of projectiles toward the hovering spaceship.

Almost immediately, the very air within a hundred feet glittered with internal atomic explosions. Little motes danced prismatically, beautifully, and seemed to be sucked toward the humans—toward the Nazis who operated the gun. Swept toward them and was helplessly breathed in by them.

And they—*fell!* Fell on the ground by the tens. And then by the hundreds, as the beam flicked toward other firing units, and still others.

And an hour passed. Bill didn't know how the Americans and British felt, but he could guess. For all along that fifty-mile battle-line, a strange cylindrical ship was moving, and a mighty army, certain of victory, was being plunged into the maddest kind of panic.

The very air surrounding every enemy unit, every tank and foxhole and pillbox, was turned to a deadly gas—which dropped men like flies!

And the Allies, grim men in olive drab, were rushing in to consolidate those miraculously harmless positions. It was probable that they had by this time seen the ship from space, and knew it was responsible. It was also probable, that by this time, the news concerning the ship from space had already been printed in innumerable newspapers, and by this time was being broadcast over the radio. But Bill was too fascinated to pick up such a broadcast from Bess-Istra's *tele-*radio.

At the end of the second hour, Bill was weak and limp from excitement. "Thank God for small favors, Johnny," he whispered. "It's done. Can you imagine it? The biggest German army ever assembled in one spot—*and it's out of commission.*"

"I have already thanked God," the young missionary stated. "Nor do I think, Bill, that it was a small favor. What we have seen is the real beginning of the end. We can win no greater victory—for this is victory. Peace will soon come to the planet Earth."

CHAPTER SEVEN
The Capture of Adolph Hitler

AND never in the history of the world was a war ended so quickly and so bloodlessly.

MUSSOLINI FLEES ROME!

Aboard The Ship From The Stars, July 19—(CF)—Today an era ends. A Fascist tyrant who became the military tool of the most hated man in the world is in disorganized retreat from the seat of his hoped-for empire.

This morning I saw the complete conquest of the German army stemming the advance of Allied troops into Italy. That news has already been flashed to the world: how the gas-ray, the utterly strange weapon of another world, rendered the Nazi forces helpless; how the Allies, suffering from almost certain defeat, swept toward Rome on the tide of certain victory; and by late tomorrow, I assure you, will have spread their rule over all of Italy.

But at noon today, through the mysterious Tele-ray of Bess-Istra, I searched out Mussolini himself, saw him sitting in session extraordinary with his ministers. The session ended with a nerve-wracked man's complete nervous collapse. His ministers were little better off. I followed them as they ran from the chamber, took a private car for the airfield, where they boarded a transport plane.

They are in that plane now—bound for Germany, like dogs running home to their master.

"And where shall we attack next, O Bill?" inquired Bess-Istra. The faint insolence on her lips lingered as a taunting reminder to Bill that he was playing with dynamite merely by standing so close to her.

As the planet Earth might be playing with dynamite by accepting her favor?

He broke off the momentary thought with a deep shudder that shook his very soul.

In answer to her question, he spoke again, gutturally, "To the Russian front..."

And to the Russian front went the ship from the stars. Went there—and left again within an hour and a half. And behind it was a German army of soldiers whose eyes were suddenly blank with lost memories.

Guns dropped from their hands.

They wandered aimlessly on the blood-drenched ground south of the River Don.

Half-track tractors hauling 155-mm howitzers, captured from the Russians earlier in the war, continued to move—but their bearded, unutterably bedraggled drivers gazed stupidly at the controls until the engines of war crashed into a tree or rolled down into a culvert and turned over.

Tanks kept on going, witlessly, until they turned over, pawing at the air with their madly clanking caterpillar treads.

Artillery ceased to fire when gunner crews sat down on the ground and picked preoccupiedly at their nails.

Transports crossing the Baltic loaded with men stopped after awhile and drifted, for the black gang no longer remembered such things as coal and engines and boilers; and the captains on the bridge merely stood and looked dumbly at the bluish fog that rolls on the Baltic swells...

And later, along the German-fortified west coast of Europe, men also turned dumb as from the ship of Bess-Istra came a high-frequency vibration that short-circuited mental synapses; or were stricken into unknowing slumber as the gas-ray got in its work.

From the north the Russians came. From the south, the American and British Allied forces. And from the west, Great Britain launched an invasion of France and Norway; and met no resistance.

Three armies swept toward Berlin as internal revolution broke...

The day of Adolph Hitler was over. As was the day of Hirohito.

"ASIA offers no greater problem," spoke Bill van Astor-Smythe grimly. "Japan has bitten off more than she can chew in China. China is not conquered—hardly occupied. Oh, the cities and villages and hamlets have been taken along the coast, and far inland. Chunking has fallen. *But*—holding a city doesn't mean that you hold the land surrounding that city. There are the guerrilla fighters who rule the open spaces between the cities, who harass Japanese troop movements and communication lines and have given the Japanese Command quaking nerves. All we have to do is to render the enemy in those cities powerless so that the native citizens and the guerrillas can overthrow them. But...how?"

Bess-Istra drew her dark brows frowningly down toward her gold-flecked eyes. "Well?" she demanded. "Sab-Hallo—how?"

The squat scientist's wide-set eyes held hers with a studied impatience. He said acidly, "There is no problem, if we but sweep such cities with psychotic waves that will set Japanese and Chinese against each other, and provide ample advantage for the guerrillas to enter and take command."

She took a step toward him, her hand falling to the gun at her hip. She said tonelessly, "This war will be ended so that we do not kill either friend or enemy, Sab-Hallo..."

"Friends!" the scientist cried, sweeping the Reverend John Stevens and Bill van Astor-Smythe with a scathing look. "They are not your—"

"Cease, Sab-Hallo!"

The command did not come from Bess-Istra, but from Bandro. The tall man's eyes were flashing with anger. He thundered at Sab-Hallo, "It is not your place to question our mistress! She is right, of course. We shall bring peace to this planet—peacefully."

The fire died from Sab-Hallo's broad face. There was a moment of silence while his eyes searched Bandro's. And Bill could have sworn that something flickered between them, some *understanding.*

Sab-Hallo's shoulders fell in resignation. "Very well, Mistress Bess," he said smoothly. "I have a weapon that will vanquish these Japanese so that the guerrillas can come in without chance of harm. The fire-ring."

By the end of that day, Bill had another story to write.

From the belly of the ship, as it hovered over a village, a swiftly expanding fire-ring was hurled; much as a smoke-ring is puffed from the throat. This fire-ring grew, both in size and in brilliance—and it dropped over the Japanese-controlled village as a cowboy would drop a noose over a running horse's head.

And like the noose of a riata, the fire-ring began to contract.

It contracted slowly. Bill saw shopkeepers come bursting from their doors in mad excitement as the ring rolled along the ground toward them; saw Japanese soldiers, darting through the streets, Japanese who knew that this was another strange weapon released from that ship that had paralyzed their allies in Europe.

There was panic in the village. The ring swept through solid structures without harm, rolled on its way unimpaired.

Neither Chinese nor Japanese dared to get near that ring, nor to hurdle it. Consequently, they were all huddled in the center of the city in a tight knot, unable to flee anywhere.

The ring came on; some Chinese leaped in it—without harm! But before others could follow their example, the fiery ring contracted to its center, rolling through the huddled people—and winked out.

Apparently nothing had happened.

BUT something had. For suddenly the vastly more numerous townspeople attacked the Japanese, probably feeling that since this was a weapon, it had been used for their benefit. And they were right. For as the Japanese soldiers attempted to fight back, their guns did not fire.

The ring of fire's only function—but a powerful one—was to eat up and to entirely dissipate a chemical without which gunpowder is not gun-powder; the ring had simply destroyed all the sulfur in that village!

By the end of that day, fire-rings had been looped over Shanghai, Hong Kong—and Singapore…

Outnumbered Japanese were swarmed over, made prisoner, and a liberated Asia started to go mad with joy. And in Tokyo, when a shining, cylindrical ship floated with the nonchalance of complete confidence over that city, high officials realized that the game had run its course. The members of that diabolical society known as the "black dragon" committed hara-kiri down to the last man.

In Australia, Japanese morale was broken, and the army that had gained a foothold on the north coast retreated with dreadful losses, and that same day was utterly destroyed when the transports on which they sought to make their escape were sunk by American B-24's.

In Java, the natives rose in one savage wave of revolt and swept over their hated conquerors. The French East Indies again raised the French flag.

Bill directed Bess-Istra in this supreme undertaking that enveloped the whole world, and literally knocked from under them the legs of the would-be totalitarian conquerors of the world. And now, as a crashing finale, he made his last suggestion, which Bess-Istra indulgently acted upon.

In Tokyo, an utterly black beam speared down from the belly of the ship, plunged through the roof of a building decorated with hideous gargoyles, sought its way down through level after level, and touched a man cowering against the wall; swallowed him up, so that there was no trace of him.

The beam snapped to another corner of the city, sought out another toothsome, wrinkled yellow man; similarly swallowed him.

The ship snapped halfway around the world in the small part of a minute. Down the black beam dipped; again, again, and again! Plunged into the very heart of the council chamber where sat a fat, cruel man, and a slim man, and a man with a large jaw, and a man with a lock of hair hanging down over his ghastly pale forehead. And others, of lesser import. These the beam swallowed.

And in a chamber in the ship, after they had been materialized there, after they had been drawn like formless gases upward through walls by the black beam, were more than a dozen men.

All-important leaders of the Axis combine were prisoners of Bess-Istra.

CHAPTER EIGHT
Mistress of Earth

IN SPITE of the fact that Bill had been in on the ground floor of a real miracle from heaven, he was stunned. So much had happened in the last few days that it was beyond the imagination to comprehend.

The war was over!

"The war is over," Bill repeated blankly. "Johnny? Did you hear me, boy?"

"Eh? Eh? Oh, yes…"

Bill's typewriter played a slow, stuttering tune, and then went like mad.

"The folks at home don't have to feel like fifth-columnists if they drink more than one and two-tenths cups of coffee. Boy! They don't have to steal extra lumps of sugar from restaurants. Huzzah! There aren't any more of those Tirpitz subs snaking along through the seas. They gave up the fight yesterday when they heard about Hitler. Poor, poor Hitler. Come here, Hitler—giffs, candy und ice cream. Come here—and I'll smash your face in. But you ought to be glad *we've* got you. You ought to be glad you're not in Berlin, what with the Tommies swarming all over the place. Hmm. Same goes for Tojo and his thugs. Too bad about Laval and Quisling. They couldn't take it—Johnny, I heard that over the *tele*-radio. Laval and Quisling picked out some real high buildings and jumped; *squerrooch!*" Bill laughed a little bit insanely. He picked at his nails with his teeth, staring at the typewriter as he tried to finish a story that would be radioed to his syndicate by Bess-Istra's equipment.

He didn't hear any answering laugh from Stevens, though.

He turned around. His jaw fell. *"Johnny!"*

"I think I can do it," Stevens whispered. His chest rose and fell. He panted, "I *know* I can..."

He jumped up and wildly paced the length of the room. His eyes were wide and staring, his lips were working over each other in a highly nervous exaltation. Bill gulped, shook his head, blinked.

"Hold it... What gives?"

"I can do it," Stevens whispered.

"Do what?"

"I can convert Bess-Istra."

"Convert—" Bill yelled the word out, and then sank back, feeling as if the world were coming to an end. He leaned forward and bared his teeth. *"Why?* Why in the name of God do you want to convert her? She's got her own religion. She's got her own system of theogony. She wouldn't want to be converted."

"Oh, yes, she would," Stevens whirled. "And why would I wish to convert anybody except in the name of God? We have been commanded to go to all corners of the Earth and preach the gospel—"

"This isn't a corner of the Earth. It's a God-forgotten piece of a planet which existed so many years ago you can't think it."

"Nothing is God-forgotten. Particularly Bess-Istra. She proves it by listening to me. By asking me about the Lord. She never tires. Bill—Bill—" Stevens' voice suddenly stopped; a stricken look appeared in his eyes. His lips shook and he bit at them. He sank down on the three-legged chair, hands between his knees. "Bill," he whispered. "Bill—*she is so unutterably lovely...*"

BILL started to say something, and the words jammed in his throat.

He jumped to his feet, holding his head in his hands, taking three long strides to the other end of the featureless room, then whirling and confronting Stevens with pity in his eyes.

"You poor hopeless idiot. You're in love with her!"

Stevens looked up and there was nothing but a blurred pain in his ingenuous blue eyes.

"I am," he choked miserably. "I am…"

"You fool. She's been leading you on. She's no more interested in your creed than that sneaking Bandro and Sab-Hallo. She likes the idea of twisting you around her little finger. She likes to pull guns on people. She likes to kick them around. There's nothing good and true in a carload of her. Convert her? Don't make me laugh. Johnny—" He paused in pained, hopeless exasperation; and then whirled as he heard a voice behind him.

"It is interesting to know in what light you regard me, O Bill…"

Bill started to speak; then clamped his lips. "You heard me," he said brutally, his glance hard on Bess-Istra.

There was cold fire in her eyes. Her skin was white as marble, and her voice bit like shattered glass shards.

"I will remember that, Bill," she grated. "I will remember that though I have freed your planet from a terrible bondage, you feel no gratitude. You feel that I have an ulterior motive instead."

A hard, accusing little smile wrinkled the corners of Bill's mouth. "I've been playing my cards as I got them, Bess-Istra. Playing them for all they were worth. And letting the finesse take care of itself. Unfortunately, I can't finesse. I've been having fun up to this point, but after this…well, Bess-

Istra…" his voice ground out the words, *"…just what is your motive?"*

"You've freed the world, you've stopped a big war, you've got the trouble-makers locked up tight. Fine. Swell. That's what you promised to do. But how come you came to this planet in a ship loaded to the gunwales with the instruments of war? How come you left your own planet at all? Who are you? What comes after this? Don't hand me that line about us being your friends. You've been playing a little game and having a lot of fun—like giving candy to children. Only maybe the candy will give us a tummy ache…"

Stevens' hand bit into Bill's arm. But all he could do was to shake his head miserably.

The color had entirely left Bess-Istra's face. Every muscle in her body was visibly tensed. Her shoulders literally shook when she spoke; and her voice jangled horribly.

"You will regret that, Bill. You will understand how you have misjudged Bess-Istra—some day. Know then, that in a few minutes from the control room of this ship I shall broadcast a message to the peoples of Earth, a message that will clear everything else from the air, a message that will sound from every open receiver in the world.

"The peoples of Earth shall soon know my intentions with regard to them—*and so shall you.*"

TWO of Bess-Istra's mechanics fiddled in the interior of the *tele*-radio that filled one side of the control room. Monstrous blurpings came from the machine. Bill knew that the ether waves of Earth were being cleared. Every station in the world literally scoured off the air by a controlled static.

Then the transmitter was ready!

Bill stood silently, his heart a stone in his breast. What would Bess-Istra say? Would she prove herself to be what Bill thought her—or what he wanted her to be?

Bess-Istra stepped in front of the grating that would receive her voice.

Her glance passed over Bandro, in whose mottled dark eyes Bill saw a hard, watchful eagerness; and then to Sab-Hallo, who stood with arms crossed on his barrel-chest, face expressionless, yet sardonic.

Lastly, Bess-Istra looked at Bill. At the icy rage in her glance, Bill flinched; but his jaw came out, and he managed to show some of his bitter cynicism in his own eyes. Slowly her lips tensed, and with a pantherine motion she twisted savagely to face the "mike," she made a motion to a nondescript man, her announcer:

"Peoples of Earth, listen... Peoples of Earth, Bess-Istra, your benefactor, shall speak to you—*now.*" The man's deep voice rolled out over the world; then he stepped aside, and Bess-Istra spoke:

"I am Bess-Istra. Know my voice, now, peoples of Earth, for you shall hear it often. I came from the stars, and found a planet in thrall, wrapped in the toils of a monstrous war, cruelly beset by creatures whom you call Nazis and Japanese; creatures whom I believe to be scarcely human. Seeing this, I at once set about freeing you.

"And now you *are* free.

"Already, by listening to the many broadcasts that fill the air-waves, I can sense the mad, hysterical joy that has taken possession of you. The war is over! The enemy is humbled, and everywhere Allied soldiers—the gallant Tommies and Yanks and Aussies and Canadians and Filipinos and Senegalese and Fighting French and innumerable others— have flowed into the conquered areas. The morale of a bewildered enemy has been hopelessly shattered. There will be no more resistance!

"These things you know. These things your great Churchill and Stalin and Roosevelt and Chiang Kai-shek have already told you.

"*But*—but, Peoples of Earth, already I sense a new conflict growing amongst you. It is not yet evident to the senses of any but one who is able to look upon the situation without prejudice—myself, Bess-Istra... I see a new monster rising amongst you—and that monster is...*indecision*.

"What shall you do with your world, now? What shall you do with the conquered peoples? How will you rebuild? Who shall acquire what territories? *What shall you do with Hitler?*"

BESS-ISTRA'S voice dropped a tensed note. Bill stiffened, a sudden hollow fear growing in his mind. What was she saying? What was she planning to do?

As if she knew he was asking the question, Bess-Istra's gold-flecked eyes locked with his, filled with a taunting, controlled rage that was directed at Bill. Then she spoke again, almost hissing the words out, they were so clearly articulated:

"These are the questions that will rise amongst you, and cause an ill-feeling that may never be erased. Therefore, peoples of Earth..." the girl from the stars drew a deep breath that shivered the clustered diadem of jewels on her breast, "...I am going to solve these problems for you!"

Bess-Istra's arm raised high, and she cried, "Peoples of Earth, know that I, Bess-Istra, now take control of the planet Earth. Know that I am your new ruler; know that I, with my irresistible ship, having freed you, now take my reward: People of Earth, your planet is—!"

Bill never knew what happened. Not much of it, anyway. His brain snapped. Broke. A purple flame shot sky-high across his vision. Perhaps he screamed. Perhaps not. But suddenly he found himself face to face with Bess-Istra, his hands outstretched like claws. He vaguely saw Bandro leaping toward him. Saw Sab-Hallo's jaw fall. And then saw Bess-Istra step back one step, pulling at the gun on her curving hip. Bill knew it was the spastic gun, which could kill so completely. He didn't care. He tried to get the gun, and the gun raised, and behind him he heard the Reverend John Stevens crying, "Bill! *Bill!*" in an agonized voice, and then little lights winked in the gun…and Bill fell!

Fell, knotted up, brain scalded with burning thoughts, and traveled interminably through a warped tunnel of pain.

And was sharply unconscious.

CHAPTER NINE
In Captivity

HE CAME out of it, fighting, yelling, squirming with an unbearable nightmare. Hands were on his arms, strong arms held him down. He relaxed. His eyes snapped opened. The drawn face of the Reverend John Stevens looked down at him.

"Bill..." Stevens choked. "Oh you were right—*right!* She never had the good of the world in mind at all. She just brought peace to the world so that she could take over more easily."

His face was twisted with the unmatchable pain of young love betrayed.

"Courage," whispered Bill. "Stiff upper lip. And all that sort of thing."

His thoughts were colder than dry ice. And as brittle. He could speak normally, and flippantly, and he could sit up now, locking his arms around his knees, sighing bleakly, and looking around at their prison. A dark prison with a grated door stingily admitting checkered light from the corridor lights outside.

His lips settled into a savage humor. He locked eyes with Stevens.

"You lost your head, too, Johnny?"

"Yes...I just couldn't stand by. And after all, I was so bitterly—so bitterly disappointed." He could speak no more and bowed his head.

Bill grasped his arm in a single strong, comforting squeeze. He shook his head slowly back and forth, in profound amazement. "We should have known, Johnny. Boy, were we the uckersays. Why didn't you stick to your guns? You thought she was a devil in the first place, until—"

"Until she told us she was going to bring peace to the world," Stevens whispered hopelessly. "I didn't think—I didn't have any reason to think there might be another purpose behind it, Bill. She—"

"Skip it. I was almost taken in myself. I *was* taken in, I guess. But I was so enthusiastic about ending the war, that I sort of figured we'd get that out of the way, get the world to perking happily again, and then somehow we could deal with Bess-Istra, if she was as dangerous as I thought she might be. And—" suddenly he was biting at his lip, "—and I guess I was hoping that maybe she wasn't that kind of a gal. I was hoping that—well, I guess I was also hoping that she could be...converted."

Stevens looked up swiftly. His touch on Bill's arm was impulsive. "Bill," he nearly whispered. "Bill, you're in love with her, too?"

"What? Huh? *Say!*" Bill's lips curled in a black snarl. He jerked his arm away as if Stevens were contaminating it. "Don't give me any of that. Why I couldn't any more fall in love with that—that—"

He stopped, paled. Stevens was regarding him with the sad smile of a man who is very, very wise.

His shoulders fell. Slowly, as if the burden of his thoughts were weighting down his head, his eyes sought the floor and stared blurrily at nothing.

DAYS, slow days, passed. Their prison was little less than an oversize cage deep in the bowels of the ship. There were toilet facilities, two low couches with silk coverlets, and two acceleration chairs.

The latter were of course useful. Frequently, a little red light winked on above the door, accompanied by a sharp, warning bell. Then Stevens and Bill would get into the chairs, and when the ship moved, the acceleration would not hurt them.

The ship was going places and doing things. Where and what?

Questions thudded dully in Bill's brain. Bess-Istra was making herself the world's ruler, undoubtedly, consolidating her power. But what was she going to do with the world? How? And what was she going to do with Hitler? *Make friends with him?*

What was she going to do with those murderous Japanese and Nazis? *Treat them like brothers, because maybe she was like them?*

Bill jumped up, paced back and forth along the length of the room, literally chewing at his nails. He knew what he'd do with Hitler, the damned, sneaking, foul-minded bit of human filth who had brought misery and starvation and death and humiliation unbearable to millions of innocent people. Or did he know? What could you do to him? What punishment would fit the crime?

The question was as maddening as those questions concerning the ends of time and space.

Maybe you should just kill him cleanly, get him out of the way, and to heck with punishment and red tape; Hitler would be dead.

Now Admiral Tojo, There was a guy... His punishment was simple. And very slight and not to be feared by such an admirable guy. Douse him in gasoline, touch him off with a safety match or a chromium-plated cigarette lighter, and chase him up and down the street. Japanese soldiers did that to the Chinese, and if the poor Chinese could take it, Admiral Tojo certainly could—

"I'm going nuts…"

"You are taking it too hard, Bill," Stevens said in distressed tones. "If you would—"

"If I would sit down and pray? I'll leave it to you, Johnny. But I want some information. If only that guard who brings us our food would talk."

"Perhaps he does not know the English tongue."

"Nuts to that. I'm telling you he does. So does every other soldier that Bess-Istra brought along from that damnable planet of hers. Bess-Istra had Bandro or Sab-Hallo put one of those helmet things on and transfer his knowledge of the tongue to a soldier who in turn taught others in the same way, and so on. Sure, they know the English language. 'Cause why? Because Bessy is going to use them in ruling the world."

The red light above the door suddenly winked. The warning bell rang. Bill hopped into his acceleration chair with a curse. Stevens followed.

They sat there for a few minutes. Then a blue light glowed, and a piping whistle sounded. The ship was motionless again. And where were they?

Who knew? They might even be out in space.

THEY weren't, though. Two weeks passed, two weeks of maddening inactivity to Bill. He was essentially an active type, active of body and mind. Neither found profitable exercise in that cage. But at the end of those two weeks, there were double footsteps in the corridor without. The guard swung the door open, admitted the person with him, and then closed the door with a bang, and rested a slim shining weapon in the grating, pointing it accurately at Bill while he faced—Bess-Istra!

His heart went out to her, impulsively—until he remembered. Her beauty, her lips which he felt could have been tender, the quality of strength, feminine strength that was wholesome, deep in her eyes, evident in her firmly set jaw, the glorious perfection of her body that was meant for the arms of a husband—these things he must ignore. He must remember only what she really was.

"Well?" said Bill. "How's your little planet getting along?"

"It is late at night, Bill."

"I should be sleeping then. Guess we'll go to bed so our company can go home. Goodnight!"

Her eyelids flickered. She said, in a small, tight voice, "Bill, I have come to you because I need your help."

He said dryly, "Uh-huh. What's the matter? Did Hitler escape? Or have you cozied up to him? Maybe you two would make a good pair."

He could have cut his tongue out as soon as he said it. He noticed now that there were dark circles under her eyes; noticed lines of strain about her mouth. But she said nothing to the accusation.

"Hitler," she said, "is being tried along with all his friends and Axis partners at a newly-formed World Court—tried in what is known as the "democratic" manner. And every German and every Japanese and every Italian who ever performed an atrocity on any innocent person, and against whom any evidence can be found, will similarly be tried."

"You don't say?" Bill suddenly began to feel slightly crazy. "And where did you get that idea?"

She frowned at him. "It was a promise made by the President of the United States long before I came to the planet of your God the Lord."

"I told her about it," Stevens broke in dully.

"Well..." said Bill. "Well, well, well. Let me get this straight, Bess-Istra. Are you the ruler of the world?"

She studied him with eyes that suddenly grew alive again with insolence.

"This planet, O Bill, is mine," she cried. "And I *am* its ruler. I am the supreme head of all governments. And the heads of those governments are merely figure heads who must take orders from me, must abide by my decisions, on pain of punishment."

"Have any of them," Bill asked with a twisted smile, "failed to cooperate with you so far?"

"No...they dare not. They know my power. They have transmitted my orders to their inferiors. The battle fleets of the world are now in dry dock under my orders. They are being scrapped—scrapped down to the destroyer. And that scrap is being used to supply industry. And all the aircraft of the world are being scrapped also."

BILL eased himself into the acceleration chair because he felt he had to sit down. He tapped on the arm of the chair for a long moment before he spoke again. His face was a study.

He said, "Doesn't a prosperous world need ocean liners—passenger planes? Couldn't those battlewagons and bombers be converted into commercial vehicles?"

Her hands were on her hips in scorn. "No....there will be no antiquated means of transportation on my world, Bill. Hereafter, trade shall be carried on with huge transports, which work on the principle of light-thrust—the same principle that impelled this spaceship across a void unutterable. Nor will I tolerate the outworn mode of currency. Already, an international currency, which I have devised with the help of certain well-known economists, is in the first stages of development.

"Already, false trade barriers such as tariffs have been outlawed. And the geography of the world is being rearranged, Bill, according to racial groups, to languages, to traditional backgrounds. That continent which you call Europe will be divided into nine distinct nationalities—only nine. Each country will be of sufficient strength, possess sufficient natural resources, that it need never fear an aggressor nation."

"Boy," said Bill, looking askance at her. "You sure do walk where angels fear to tread! Or maybe they haven't walked there because they couldn't. Too much red tape. But the dictator tramples over many conventions, eh?"

And she said serenely, "I have accomplished many things, Bill. I am remaking the outworn social pattern of the planet of your God the Lord—remaking it according to what I conceive would be His wishes."

Bill was staggered. He could have been no more winded if somebody had jolted him in the stomach. He didn't believe it. It was beyond the realm of common sense. She was a lying, cheating hellcat, and anybody with a grain of brain cells would know it. So why couldn't he tell her so?—in spite of the almost childishly pleased expression she wore?

But he couldn't. He was going to be a fool and fall for it.

Nor could Stevens. Nor did Stevens want do. Stevens was like a man who suddenly sees the sun where there had been only palling cumulus heaps.

"Mistress Bess..." he cried, his face radiantly transfigured. "You mean you believe—you believe in that which I have told you?"

For a moment there was a flicker in her eyes. Then she nodded solemnly. "Yes...I believe. I believe in your God the Lord. The principles he lays down seem very efficient."

Stevens tried to speak, and choked up. Bill got embarrassed.

"Okay, okay, okay... So she believes." He was inwardly fuming, alive with cynicism. He blazed, "Skip it. Let's get down to your real purpose, Bess-Istra. You came here…why?"

"For your help."

"What kind of help?"

HER eyes dropped. Her fingers twisted together. "The readers of your column in many newspapers have been clamoring for your return, O Bill. And I wish you to return. And this time, I wish you to dwell on—well, to dwell more on me as subject matter, instead of the great things that I do."

Bill's hands went to his hips. He laughed a short, barking laugh. "A press agent?" he cried scornfully.

"Yes. I want you to write me down as one who loves his fellow men."

Bill looked at Stevens. "Hi, there, Abou ben Adam!" He turned back to Bess-Istra. "But why do you need somebody to extol your virtues when you've already squelched a man-sized war? The people probably worship you, don't they?"

"No…" A bleak dread grew in her eyes, a humid mistiness of sudden bewilderment. "Bill, somehow there is a traitor in my own camp. A traitor who is giving information concerning me to the newspapers. Who is trying to turn the people of the world against me. And who is succeeding…"

"Because…" Bill said, staring into her piercing gold-flecked eyes clear to the roots of her brain, "…it's *true*?"

"True? True?" Her eyes took fire. "Of course it is true—but the people misinterpret. They do not realize—"

Bill wearily ran his hand through his crisp dark hair. He shook his head in long helpless arcs. "And I'll wager that Hitler is screaming his head off right now in that World Court, saying that people don't understand. This is nuts! Listen, Bess-Istra…"

He took a stance, his face hard.

"I'm going to take that press-agenting job—and I'll turn out plenty of guff for the world to slop up. But layoff the Pollyanna act when you're around me. Don't go out of your way to show Johnny and me how religion changed your life— because you know and I know that it didn't. Get it? Okay…let me at my typewriter."

He started toward the door.

And Bess-Istra struck him. Lashed at him with the full force of her palm. Brought him to an utter, confounded standstill.

"Beast!" she cried. "Pig!"

She kicked him in the shins, at the same time raised her hand. The door opened. She stepped into the corridor. She turned and spoke angrily to Stevens, "Come, Johnny. There are more truths that I would learn from you concerning the ethics of your religion."

She moved down the corridor, tiny bells on the hem of her short garment jangling to the rhythm of her step.

Stevens stared after her like a man shocked. Then he went out the door—like a moth that is soon to be devoured by the flame?

Bill stood there, fists knotted.

"Do that again, Bess-Istra," he vowed very softly through his teeth, "and it gives—*murder.*"

CHAPTER TEN
Treachery

AS THE weeks, the months passed, Bill van Astor-Smythe was glad that he had taken his job—for *Bess-Istra literally changed the world.*

Changed it, utterly remade it.

Sab-Hallo, the squat scientist, was put in charge of industry. Soon, all airplane plants and shipyards were turning out great transports that moved by the unique principle of light-thrust; were engaged in manufacturing small, one-man "gliders," which really weren't gliders at all, but motorized craft on which the driver lay at full length.

New methods of mining were introduced. A new kind of power-machine was developed that harnessed free energy formed by the rotation of Earth's magnetic field through space. A weather machine was tested by Sab-Hallo, and was turned out in large quantities. There would never again be famine on the planet Earth! Climate could be controlled.

All over the world the illustrious change took place. China was reborn, as modern industrial machinery flowed in to take the place of laboring coolies. And the Chinese did not suffer because the machines took only a few minutes to do what formerly took hours; their standard of living was simply raised, their leisure time increased. And so it was, over the whole world.

Bess-Istra ruthlessly discarded outmoded systems of government. Expensive and useless bureaus were dispensed with.

The world was rebuilt. A new London, glowing lustrous, raised on the ruins of the old. Scorched earth was treated with chemicals that made it productive again.

Bess-Istra, seeking for some means to keep order in the world, created an International Police, with Bandro as the Chief Officer. The thousand soldiers she brought with her were recruited for their duties in this organization. On the breast of each was the symbol of Bess-Istra—the blood-red scimitar. And "Scimitars" was what this International Police force came to be known as.

Bill didn't get along with Bandro; nor with Sab-Hallo for that matter. He didn't trust either of them. He didn't like the idea of those two having so much power. Bandro and his Scimitars could be a terrifically dangerous power in the world.

Bill mentioned this to Bess-Istra, but he didn't get very far with it. A hostility existed between Bess-Istra and him that—while it never broke through to the surface—laid dormant like a slumbering volcano.

Sometimes Bill was convinced that Bess-Istra hated him with violent passions, that she still remembered his denouncement of her. At other times, he was almost inclined to believe that she sought to get under the hard shell of indifference in which he clothed himself when she was around. At times she was tender, almost yielding. And at such times it was hard to restrain himself. He was convinced she was a devil girl from the stars—but sometimes his desire for her was almost overwhelming. And he hated himself for it.

BILL watched the actions of the Reverend John Stevens with a smoldering eye. Stevens now was pastor of the largest church in Washington...in his denomination. His fame had apparently been such these past weeks that he was offered the post. But in between times, Stevens was apparently trying to convert Bess-Istra to his faith.

"Grow up," Bill said wrathfully.

"You were practically a kid as far as brains went when I picked you up in the jungle. Now that you've gotten loose in the world, you're running wild. Falling in love with that…"

"But—but she—"

"She *nothing*. I'm beginning to get an idea about that gal. Think it's religion that's making her remake the world? Nuts. One of these days we'll all wake up and discover that we'd be better off if we were still peacefully making war with Hitler. Oh…I'll keep on playing the game, and being fairly happy, and I'll let myself be lulled into security just like everybody else. But after that—" He slid his finger pictorially across his throat.

Stevens helplessly shook his head. "Bill—Bill there can be nothing deceitful about her. I know."

"Hmmm." Bill was morose. "Wait until things begin to crack—you'll change your mind."

But in spite of these occasional black thoughts, it seemed to Bill that Utopia was indeed on the way.

He marveled at it openly, convincing himself all over again that Bess-Istra was on the up and up. But Bill knew that he was somewhat responsible for these brightening prospects. His articles swept the world from pole to pole. He turned out reams of material in which Bess-Istra was the utterly desirable heroine.

Bess-Istra visits the poor and promises the world that the era of poverty has come to an end…

Bess-Istra takes to her sick bed after an exhausting conference with the great men of the world—a conference that will cure more of humanity's woes than all similar conferences of the hundred years just past…

Bess-Istra is offered a screen role by Metro-Goldwyn-Mayer, the offer turned down because Bess-Istra wants to serve her people...

To Bill's credit, most of the items were basically true. But sometimes he distorted them to a sob-sister angle. And he knew that her popularity was becoming enormous.

Even a dictator such as Bess-Istra needed the support of the people.

But—and it was like the ominous clang of a muted cymbal—someone was trying to undermine the good will the people felt toward Bess-Istra. Articles concerning her past were being published openly. Bill suspected that Bandro was behind it; but he said nothing.

And one day, with an appalling rush, the overfilled dam of events...*broke!*

Bess-Istra faced him that day and said gravely, "I will not suppress the news, O Bill, because this is a world of free speech. It is a democratic world."

"You're a funny one, Bess-Istra," he said. "You're a dictator, with unlimited power. You rule a planet that is alien to you. Yet you act sometimes as if you actually give a damn about the people of this planet, when anybody with any sense at all knows that the only love which impels you is the love of power. Just as the articles that some papers print accuse you of a base love of power, and reveal events on that other planet, which must make you cringe. Why *don't* you stop those articles? I would if I had the power. I'm interested in making people *love* you."

THEY stood facing each other in the lavishly colored suite of a white plastic building from which Bess-Istra administered the affairs of a world. Bill was dressed in a cellu-suit that looked and felt like nub tweed, but as a matter of fact it was a certain grade of paper. Bill had paid one unit of currency for it, which amounted to about sixty cents of the old money. Tonight Bill would throw it in a boiler and run the suit down the drain and tomorrow would put on another suit.

There was nothing humble about Bess-Istra. She carried herself with an imperious dignity, carried herself like a ruler. But more than once she had taken Bill's outright insults without more than a hardening of her perfect lips.

"*Do* they love me, Bill?" she grated.

"Naturally. But would they if I didn't play you up as a goddess in your own right?"

"Yes!" She blazed out the word, taking a step toward him. "They would see beneath everything, and would know that I think of them. John knows, Bill. It was he who showed me the light. It was he who—oh, Bill!"

He was amazed to see the hot emotion drain from her glorious features; amazed to see the flood of tears that washed suddenly from her eyes. And somehow, he would never know in what manner, he was very close to her, enough to feel the warmth of her body, to see the throbbing pulse in her creamy throat. Her eyes were half-closed, and her lips were up-raised.

Bill was held rooted, with a hopeless passion. Oh, damn, and double damn. Why did things have to happen this way? She was an alien woman, and God only knew what alien thoughts might go on in her mind. What was her purpose in acting like this? Or was there a purpose?

"Oh, Bill," she whispered, and a sob caught in her throat, "only you do not know—you and Bandro and Sab-Hallo, who think me wicked."

Who thought her wicked? And why not? Hadn't Bill read about her struggle for power on another planet? How she had enslaved millions, geared them to a world order meant to satisfy her every whim?

And yet—Bill ground his teeth on the paradoxical thought—on *this* planet she had so far exhibited none of that cruelty.

He looked down at her parted lips, at her face that was wrenched by a kind of childish misery. He knew with horrible knowledge, that it must be as Stevens said—that he was beginning to love her! Beginning to love her in spite of the fact that she had toyed with the affections of her arch-enemy, the prime minister of another planet, who had overthrown her; in spite of the accusations made against her in anonymous newspaper articles that she had...murdered! In spite of her conquest and enslavement of the people of another planet, so that she might satiate her base lust for power.

He groaned abjectly. It was useless. She was like a child, bewilderment of some kind eating acidly at her soul. Some alchemy had taken place in her, and she was altogether lovable—

"Bess-Istra!" he choked humbly. "Oh, Bess...Bess..."

His hands closed about her soft shoulders. He drew her fiercely toward him, crushed her lips to his—or tried to!

AT THE last second, he sensed with awful foreknowledge her treachery—her deceit! Her eyes opened widely. A laugh tinkled from deep within her being as she thrust herself away from him, took a stance a few feet away, her whole mien changed to one of living scorn.

"Fool!" she said. "Utter fool for believing you could capture the love of Bess-Istra. Now you suffer. From the first, you had no kind word for me—treated me at once like one who is to be spat upon."

She burst into a wild laugh while his face was drenched in a ghastly whiteness that was like the color of a corpse.

She thrust up a quivering arm, and her gold-flecked eyes flashed with savage passions that he had never before seen there.

Her voice grated, "You are a strong man, O Bill, and cynical beyond your years. You have never known real pain, the pain that I have known—when I was a slave-girl in the Temple of Stuz, and the priests of cruelty reviled me as you have reviled me. But now you will know pain—pain that will endure in you forever—"

Bill strode forward. "The pain that endures in Johnny Stevens, witch," he blazed, outraged beyond reason.

He would have killed her. Would have killed her though she had drawn her ever-present spastic gun; for as he advanced, with his hideous purpose written clear on his face, she fell back one step, then two. He heard the controls of the spastic-gun, the deadly weapon, clack around; knew that Bess-Istra had set the gun so that destroying vibrations would lash out.

And yet she did not pull the trigger.

Bill would have killed her, for on her face was written her inability to spray him with those deadly vibrations—her inability to murder in cold blood. He advanced on her like Colossus—but stopped dead still as a tittering burst of laughter lanced through the lustrous, glowing room.

The tittering of the scientist…Sab-Hallo! Bill had a flash of intuition, for his consuming rage must have made him super-sensitive. His nerves twanged with an abrupt dread.

He whirled—even as Bess-Istra whirled in the same direction. And both faced not only Sab-Hallo but—a full dozen of Bandro's International Police, each of whom held to the ready a squat black weapon trained squarely on Bill *and* Bess-Istra.

CHAPTER ELEVEN
Johnny Stevens, Sky-Pilot

"REMAIN still, or you die immediately…"

The squat little scientist's voice lashed out, filled with smirking undertones.

Silence held. Bill was rooted. At last came Bess-Istra's voice, robbed of moisture.

"What means this, Sab-Hallo? Disband these Scimitars at once. Know you not that I will flay you alive if your purpose be what I think it?"

But Sab-Hallo laughed a deadly little laugh.

"The days when Bess-Istra may wreak her will on others," he said venomously, "are—*done*. The days when Bess-Istra may misuse the glorious science that I, Sab-Hallo, have prepared for her, are finished."

His broad face writhed suddenly with an unnameable passion—perhaps of hate. Then it was quiet again.

"You know why we overthrow you, Mistress Bess," he said into the silence that seethed inside Bill's temples. "For we *are* overthrowing you. Often we have asked you—demanded of you that you treat the people of Earth as a conquered race must be treated. You spurned us!

"The troublesome ones who lead the Axis armies still live. *Fah* for such inefficiency. The very nations that harbor the seed of future rebellions against us continue to exist. Germany and Japan must, and shall be—destroyed.

"And now, Mistress Bess—in a few moments, you shall see how I and my confidante, Bandro, conduct a trial—*not by the democratic method.*"

"Bandro!" The word broke from the lips of Bess-Istra. Shocked bewilderment was on her face. "Bandro, who told me of his love. And you, Sab-Hallo, whom I rescued from a wretched hovel and brought to greatness. Traitors…traitors both!"

"Traitors," he agreed, and his laugh tittered out again. "But from this moment on, the planet Earth is ours to do with as we please. Technician-Scimitar, adjust the television controls to the interior of the World Court where Hitler is being endlessly tried for his deeds."

THE Technician-Scimitar broke from the massed group of International Police, approached the *tele*-radio. In another moment, there was revealed on the screen a picture of the interior of the World Court, where the villainous men who had started the war were being tried.

There was no audition, merely sight. And Bill saw Hitler. The little man was seated at a table beneath the judge's platform. It was only one of many times that Bill had thus seen Hitler, and he looked woodenly at that despicable face.

It was a mass trial, and seated near Hitler were others of the same foul breed.

"Watch," Sab-Hallo broke out softly. "Watch…the moment draws near…"

At various entrances to that square, extravagantly guarded courtroom were heavily armed International Police, with the blood-red scimitar, symbol of Bess-Istra's reign, on their shirts.

Bill knew that no faction with the possible intent of rescuing the Axis leaders could break into that courtroom.

And yet he had the conviction that something unscheduled was going to happen.

Something did.

Bill heard Bess-Istra gasp, saw Sab-Hallo's broadening grin as every Scimitar in the courthouse sprang to attention, threw open the doors, and admitted other hordes of Scimitars. They came running down the aisles and onto the rostrum where sat the dozen men who had betrayed the world.

And at their head was—Bandro!

The courtroom was thrown into pandemonium. But Bandro raised his hands, and shouted out a few sentences. The International Police drew their weapons and menaced the crowd, which had become evidently hostile.

Bandro stepped toward Hitler and the others and without warning drew two weapons, which he trained on them.

Bill found himself panting with dread. "Don't," he cried in agony. "Don't do it!"

"But he shall," ground out Sab-Hallo. "It is the only way to dispose of trouble-makers—the democratic way is outmoded! The people of Earth will soon learn that."

And suddenly it was over. Mussolini, Goering, Tojo, Hitler, and their henchmen must have realized the terrible fate in store for them. Their reactions were different. Some continued to sit, frosty-eyed. Some clattered to their feet, screaming, cowering. And as livid red bursts of flame poured toward the arch-traitors from Bandro's viciously held guns, Bill caught one glimpse of Adolph Hitler before he vanished in a puff of thick, oily smoke, saw his screaming, hideously distorted face—distorted as if in the last moment of his terrible, terrible life he suddenly understood, with a bright awful clarity, what he had done…

Smoke rolled away and where *they* had been was only formless vacancy.

The scene flicked off. Bill turned dumbly toward Sab-Hallo.

"What good will it do?" he asked through parched lips.

And Sab-Hallo drew his own weapon, a smaller variety of the flame-gun that Bandro had used.

"The same good," he said viciously, "as it will to rid the world of my Mistress Bess and of...you."

BESS-ISTRA looked at her former pawn without visible reaction. Bill knew what her thoughts were. It was evident that by giving Bandro charge of the International Police, she had literally given him control of the world. The International Police in the World Court had acted according to a pre-arranged plan.

Bandro and Sab-Hallo had held out to them rich prizes in wealth and in power; had promised them a world to loot; while Bess-Istra had insisted on keeping her soldiers to the rigid law and order demanded by democratic rule.

Bill knew whose side he was on!

But how was he to overcome this cruel, conceited toad of a man? This Sab-Hallo, who had probably been responsible for those articles intended to undermine the faith of the people in Bess-Istra?

Bandro, in spite of Sab-Hallo's declaration that Bandro was merely his pawn, was very likely the real leader of the movement, and was merely using Sab-Hallo. But Sab-Hallo had to be taken care of first.

Bill knew in his heart that it was hopeless. Even now, Sab-Hallo was about to depress the trigger, and all the glorious beauty that was Bess-Istra would be gone forever.

Bill van Astor-Smythe knew it was suicide to charge the squat scientist, but in him was the hot necessity of at least fighting and dying. Merely to die was not his idea of dignity. His muscles tensed, and—

He never jumped.

For his eyes suddenly raised to the great window at the far side of the room, a single invisible pane of glass which melted into the walls, and through which he could see the Washington Monument. And driving straight toward that pane of glass with terrific speed came one of the strange, otherworld gliders that Bess-Istra had introduced to this world.

On it came, and there was a man spread-eagled on it on his stomach, shielded from the slip stream by a conical, fanning guard of cimarite. On it came, at such an angle that neither Sab-Hallo nor his men could see it. Crashing through the window, sending shards spinning in a thousand directions. And from its nose as it halted above the heads of the whirling Sab-Hallo and his men, came—the gas-ray!

In a moment, the men who had menaced Bill and Bess-Istra's life had fallen unconscious. Sab-Hallo alone was not caught. He swore lividly and vanished out the door.

The glider landed at the far corner of the suite, where the two rescued people had run to escape any possible gas.

And the Reverend Johnny Stevens, quite literally a sky pilot, jumped from the glider!

CHAPTER TWELVE
Jungle Retreat

"JOHNNY!" Bill's relief vented itself in a scream. "You old son-of-a... Why didn't you come two minutes sooner? I almost fried of dight. I'm as white as a wheat, I mean wheat as a sheet—"

"Never mind!" Stevens cried. "Sab-Hallo has escaped. He'll bring others. We'll be pursued. Quickly!"

Bess-Istra lost no time in taking fullest advantage of a critical situation. She was onto the glider, strapping herself to one side of the broad metal center piece. Bill strapped himself beside her, and Stevens, with complete lack of ministerial dignity, threw himself atop them, grabbed the U-bar, plunged it home, and twisted it.

The glider rose like a shot, whipped around, and flung itself through the shattered window, and in another moment was boring its frantic way through the atmosphere five miles above solid ground.

The escape had been made; but death would soon be on the trail.

IT WAS not cold. It seemed as if there were warm air-currents, of normal atmosphere pressure, surrounding the strange ship. Both the warmth and the pressure were generated by the very speed of the craft's flight through the thinner air.

"A ship!" Bill suddenly cried, twisting his head around to look into the backward distance. "We're being pursued. Johnny, where are you taking this crate?"

And Stevens replied, shouting above the wind, "We're being chased, and he who chases us thinks to destroy us. And there is only one place in all this world which I truly call home."

Bill grinned widely. "Mozambique? Portuguese East Africa…your mission house?"

"Exactly. The house of the Lord. The Lord is my shepherd and he has led me into strange pastures, but now I am returning." His face, that had seemed so young, so freshly naive, now seemed inexpressibly—and sadly—older. He said austerely, "Brother…sister…the Lord our God will protect us, will fill us full of divine faith. We cannot lose."

"Hmm," Bill said, in a vaguely skeptical tone, as he saw that the furiously driven craft that pursued them was scarcely three miles distant.

Stevens explained to Bill how he had come to know that Sab-Hallo and Bandro were plotting the downfall of Bess-Istra; were going to depose her without so much as a struggle.

"As you know," he said sorrowfully, "my proximity to the adventures that have so changed the world has given me considerable notoriety. I was offered the largest church of my faith in Washington, D. C."

He stopped as Bess-Istra raised her dark head and smiled tawnily. "Because I asked that you be offered such a post."

"You?"

"Yes. Already I know what you are about to tell me. Many Scimitars attended your church. Scimitars who knew of the plot that was brewing against me. It was I who suggested that they attend the religious services with which you worship the Lord your God. A suggestion of mine is—a command. And I knew—"

"And you knew," Bill exclaimed, "that probably at least one of the Scimitars would get religion and inform Johnny about the plot. Visionary thinking! But it almost didn't work out."

And Stevens nodded soberly. "One of the Scimitars who discovered the wonderful light of the Lord told me that you and Mistress Bess were to be slain shortly. I came as quickly as I could—"

AN HOUR of driving speed followed.

Below them, the shadowy outline of Florida was lost in distance, gave way to ocean as they fled out over the Atlantic. And behind them came not one, but three of the slim, wickedly constructed light-thrust ships used by the International Police.

Death was on the trail.

Bill looked sidewise at Bess-Istra. She lay flat on her stomach. Her gloriously tinted features were calm, fully controlled. Again Bill felt an overwhelming tenderness for her—until he remembered her deceit. Then he wanted to throttle her. He ground his teeth.

Bess-Istra spoke after a long silence. "I do not think we will be able to escape from this with our lives," she said calmly.

And Stevens ground out, "We shall. We must! The peace and happiness of the whole world is at stake, Mistress Bess. Under your rule, mankind was truly progressing to a promised land. Under that of Bandro and Sab-Hallo...I shudder to think of what horror will be perpetrated."

And as if his faith truly preserved them, they made the Portuguese East African jungle, swooped down to a landing just as the three craft following them had gained to less than a thousand feet behind!

They were forced to land in that sea of foliage because from the nose of the foremost craft a cone of light was emitted.

"The green ray of destruction!" Bess-Istra panted in a dreadful voice. She unstrapped herself from the glider. "Quickly! Do as I say. The green ray will be swept over this entire strip of jungle, killing all insects, all animals, all organisms of any kind. And it will kill us unless you come very close to me—for I have a *bik!*"

"A *bik!*" cried Bill. "But I thought there were no *biks* on this planet, that there was no protection against the green ray?"

"I brought but one *bik* with me from my planet. One that I had hidden in the Citadel where I was driven by my enemies."

It was the first time she had ever made truthful reference to her past life. And Bill was amazed to see starlet tears on her lashes. But he knew now was no time to waste trying to solve this enigmatic girl. He saw clutched in her hand a tiny round metal object from which small studs protruded. She plucked at the studs—and part by part, the round ball expanded until it was a full foot in diameter, flat, however; in appearance in seemed much like a loop antenna.

"Come close," she cried, and the two men immediately moved toward her until their bodies were touching warmly. She held the *bik* between them. "It will draw the energies of the green ray much as a lightning rod draws lightning. There is only the difference that the *bik* will store those energies— and if it receives too much may explode and tear up a full mile of jungle. There! *The green ray!*"

SHE pointed with her free hand—and Bill's blood froze as he saw a light-thrust ship sweep over the massed jungle foliage, from its belly coming a thick green beam.

There was a roaring awful sound as the beam swept through the jungle scarcely thirty feet distant. And Bill immediately smelled roasted flesh—the roasted flesh of hapless creatures of the jungle.

"Missed us!"

But the ship overhead, though it could not have seen the three fugitives in the equatorial gloom, was thorough. It criss-crossed over head at tremendous speed until it seemed that the only spot in that locality that had not been touched was that where they stood huddled.

Bill hoped fiercely that the green beam would miss them. He didn't trust the *bik*.

But suddenly he knew the ray was going to touch them. It swept toward them, walking on one livid leg through the jungle. Ghastly sweat grew on his forehead; he felt Stevens and Bess-Istra tense. And then the ray was on them!

They were bathed in intolerable brilliance. The *bik* leaped with fire. And then the beam was gone—and they were alive.

After that, Bill no longer feared the ray. Seven times it swept over them before the last of the three ships that had pursued them disappeared. Then Bess-Istra dropped the *bik* to the ground; a *bik* that was crawling with energies titanic.

"We must leave—and quickly," Bess-Istra whispered. "We have no instrument which can discharge the stored energies in the *bik*. If it explodes before we are far enough away—"

The glider rose with its human load after a long, agonizing minute of preparation. It flitted slowly between the branches of squat baobab trees. They could not rise above the jungle, because they had no assurance that their enemy did not still linger. But the explosion, when it came, literally caught the glider up and threw it high into the air.

Stevens leveled it out with frantic effort—just as it was about to crash. Ghastly sweat streamed from Bill's face as the glider again floated along, smoothly. Three human beings, the hope of the world, were safe and alive.

And hope ran higher still, when Stevens brought the glider to a smooth landing in the lonely courtyard of his jungle mission.

Shock awaited them, however.

Thomas Reynolds, Stevens' assistant, was dead in the little kitchen. Around the mission grounds were a number of Bantus, also dead. Bandro's ships, not content to take chances, had swept their green rays of death over this whole section of jungle for miles and miles around. All bird, reptile, insect, and animal life had been snuffed out; probably there was no human life within a day's journey.

"Damn Bandro!" Bill whispered with bitter, tearless rage.

CHAPTER THIRTEEN
The Translation

THE days passed swiftly. Bill knew they dare not leave their retreat—not yet. For Bandro was thorough and might be on the lookout.

But by means of the *tele*-radio built into the instrument panel of the glider, they kept track of world events.

And current history was truly in turmoil—hideous turmoil. Bandro had taken over the world with a vengeance. His International Police constricted over the world like a net. Thousands upon thousands of Japanese and Nazis suspected of having performed war atrocities were executed summarily.

"Goodbye democracy," Bill gritted.

"When we abolish the trial system, no matter how heinous the crime, we abolish our whole way of life. Bandro may be doing a good thing by killing those people off. But he's not doing it for that reason. He's doing it because they might be future trouble-makers to him."

Bill and Bess-Istra were alone before the *tele*-radio. Bill turned, surprised Bess-Istra with a tear sliding down her cheek. But it was not a tear of sympathy. It was a tear of humiliation and outrage.

"Someday," she whispered, "someday when I regain control of my world again, I shall throttle Bandro with my own hands…"

"I doubt," Bill said cuttingly, "if you will ever rule Earth again, Bess-Istra."

She whirled on him. She stood in a feline crouch, and from long force of habit, her hand fell to her weapon.

"Do not say that!" she cried.

"I'll say what I damn well please," Bill told her, striding toward her. "You've pulled a gun on me once too often, lady. I was prevented from doing anything about it last time. Now it's different. *Give me that gun…*"

He wrenched it from her, threw it across the room. She burst into a strident scream of rage and flung herself at him with raking claws. He bent her wrists back, finally grasped her bare shoulders, held her rigid with steel-hinged hands.

He bit out, "You lying little beast! Actions speak louder than words. By desiring to kill Bandro you put yourself in the same class as Bandro. You've deceived me and you've deceived Johnny. All that guff about your believing in his religion…"

Her eyes grew big and round. The rosy color drained from her perfect cheeks. She whispered chokingly…

"I believe in your God the Lord."

"Our God the Lord, you should say if you meant it—which you don't."

"Our God the Lord," she blazed. "I believe in Him. I have modeled this planet according to His wishes. The people of Earth were knowing perfect peace under my rule."

"You're still too dangerous for all of that, Bess-Istra." His gaze on her was hard and penetrating, searing into her soul with pitiless knowledge.

She completely lost control. She let out several terrifying screams and kicked with her legs. He held her off, swearing bitterly under his breath. At last he spun her around, slammed her against the wall.

"You have remodeled Earth by theory," he panted, "not because you feel that what you have done is right. Superficially, you admire the God of this planet. He is something new to you. He offers a new method for you to gain power—to gain power through a selfish type of kindness. But inwardly—in your heart of hearts—*you still worship the diabolical, merciless Goddess Stuz!*"

A MORTAL pallor swept her face.

He sneered bitterly. "I know your history, Bess-Istra. I picked it up from bits you or Bandro or Sab-Hallo or some of your men let drop. And got plenty of it from some of the articles written against you. You were captured from your birthplace when still a child, were raised as a slave-girl in the Temple of Stuz. You were spat upon, reviled by the very priests of that cruel religion. Instead of hating the Goddess Stuz and what she had brought upon you, you commenced to worship her yourself—believed that in cruelty lay power—in selfish barbaric willfulness lay true contentment. And so the spat-upon slave girl began to plot how she could conquer her planet. She met Sab-Hallo, whose resourceful brain invented weapons that ravaged the planet, put her on the throne. Unfortunately, her Prime Minister did not worship the Goddess Stuz—and so, Bess-Istra, your own armies and weapons were turned against you, and you had no protection. You fled. But you *still* worship Stuz."

Bess-Istra looked at him with horrible fascination.

She said, "The Goddess Stuz must be dead—it has been so long ago—and there was a new God here—a strange God—and," she added in husky voice, "a wonderful God."

Her breasts woke to life. She panted. She cried, "I no longer worship Stuz the cruel—I love the true God—but I must kill you, O Bill, for your arrogance!"

She came like thunder and lightning, nothing more than a beast alive with terrible emotions. Bill was borne backward, shielding his face. Then his mind grew crystal clear. He threw her off balance, and while she teetered, struck her with savage fury with the flat of his hand.

She staggered back. Bill knew nothing save unutterable impatience that was like madness. He had never struck a woman before. He would never strike another woman again, ever. But he struck Bess-Istra—punishingly, once, twice, three times.

SHE slammed back against the wall. She looked at him through animal-dumb eyes, a painful confusion sweeping her face. Her legs gave way. She slid down along the wall. She crumpled up on the floor of the room, head buried in her arms.

Bill stood over her, panting.

Her body shook, soundlessly. And then with sobs. Long, racking sobs of a woman who knows an agony of mind that will never end.

Bill's voice shook violently when he spoke. He heard it through an avalanche of pounding blood in his own head.

"I shouldn't have done it, maybe. But I'm glad I did. I would have wanted someone to do it to me if it would help. Do unto others as you would have them do unto you—*that's the Golden Rule*. It embodies all tolerable religions in one form or another. The Goddess Stuz didn't know about it. And so you can't be blamed for your past on that other planet. Those people are dead anyway—dead and forgotten ages ago, along with Stuz. But now you know the *Rule, Bess-Istra*."

After awhile her sobs quieted, but she still lay there, head buried, wilted like a plucked petal. Bill left, biting at his lip. Already he regretted his action. It would do no good. Bess-Istra was Bess-Istra: Unchangeable…evil.

An hour later in the mission yard, the Reverend John Stevens quickly approached. Bill had been pacing up and down, scowling.

Rapture was on Stevens' face, a look of glorious fulfillment.

"Come," he whispered. "Quickly—you must see this."

They stood in the door of the chapel where black, fuzzy-haired African natives had worshipped a God that was new to them.

Bill shook. Kneeling at the altar, head bowed to floor level, silent and white and unmoving, was Bess-Istra. They watched her for many minutes. Finally she rose and moved down the aisle toward them. She faced them. The hard, selfish lines about mouth and eyes were gone as if they had never existed.

Her expression was so exalted, so filled with tenderness, that Bill was embarrassed. He knew without asking that Bess-Istra was—*changed!* Changed inwardly. She looked at him with a serene confidence and understanding that made him squirm.

She touched first Bill's then Stevens' hand.

"My dearest friends—Johnny—Bill—I see things with such a different light, now. So different. We must soon make plans to loose the world from the terrible bondage that has been put on it by Bandro. We three alone. Even though we may sacrifice our lives it will be well worth it if man is made free again."

Stevens looked after her with the pride of a pastor in his flock; in his glowing eyes the sight of a man in love.

Bill said softly, "Damn. Can you tie that?"

Bess-Istra's head was held high as she walked across the dusty compound, toward her room in the tiny south wing.

"Damn!" said Bill. *"She's got religion…"*

CHAPTER FOURTEEN
A Desperate Gamble

RELIGION, she had. An illustrious alchemy had taken place in her mind, and base metal was changed to gold. Her tears were real and pitying when the next shocking news came over the *tele*-radio.

Bandro sent scores of his ships filled with International Police over the cities of Tokyo and Berlin. And those ships, using every awful weapon known to that strange science, utterly killed every man, woman, and child in those cities! Utterly destroyed those cities until they were less than smoking cinder heaps.

And then proceeded indiscriminately to kill and destroy every living thing and every man-made object within a hundred miles.

Directly after this news was purveyed, Bandro spoke to the world. Bandro...dictator of Earth.

Bill was filled with revolted horror of the arch-murderer as he appeared on the television screen.

Of the silently sneering Bandro who had apparently been so subservient to Bess-Istra there was nothing left. Here was a man who was strong with the ferocity of a killer whale, and as bold.

"These people shall be punished," he cried to the world, flinging his hand up in terrible promise. "You shall learn that I will not tolerate these who brought you such horror. They and their works shall vanish. There will be unequaled prosperity on the planet Earth. And those amongst you who would menace the happiness of the others, shall be dealt with properly. And know you that my Scimitars, brave and true men, shall guard you from such plotters."

In this vein he continued, for a half-hour, subtly threatening the people to submit to his tyranny. As such Bill recognized it. His heart sank. How could they overcome this man?

The destruction of the capital cities of Germany and Japan struck them all as needless butchery. And yet Bill, thinking it over, told Stevens and Bess-Istra what he believed in his heart to be true.

"Don't pity the ruling people of those countries too much, even if Bandro does destroy them," he grated. "You should have seen Polish dead on the streets of Warsaw as I have—— kicked into the gutter by Nazis. You should have seen starving Greeks, all the flesh gone from their bodies. You should have seen the piles of Greek bodies heaped like brushwood in the city streets. You should have seen Chinese coolies used for bayonet practice by Japanese soldiers, while other Japanese stood by and learned how it was done.

"Misery of the most refined sort means nothing to these sorts of men—as long as it is not they who experience that misery. It may take more than kindness and love to change them—and maybe Bandro has the right answer..."

Bess-Istra's eyes flashed.

"No..." she cried softly. "Bandro's way will never be right, O Bill. We must take the power away from Sab-Hallo and Bandro before they plunge the world into even greater misery than the terrible Axis powers. We must!"

And if either of the two men had ever had any doubts about the change of heart that had occurred in Bess-Istra, it was dispelled now by the shining tears hanging on the edge of her lashes.

ANOTHER month passed. The three human beings lived off canned goods in the mission; and also off the cooked bodies of animals the green ray had killed.

But at the end of that month, into Bill's mind leaped the only way in which the gigantic project of freeing the world might be accomplished.

For the world was truly in the grip of a tyrant. Millions of soldiers and civilians in the conquered countries had been destroyed. Men walked in fear and trembling. Another Hitler walked the Earth. The Scimitars were but another Gestapo.

Religions had been discarded. Bandro was forcing humanity to worship...

Stuz!

Already temples to the cruel goddess were being erected.

"I am so sorry, Johnny." Bess-Istra's voice was like the sigh of the southern Trades, which blew in from the Pacific; her touch of his hand was tender. Stevens looked up gratefully from his despair.

Bill bit his lip, and forced a grin. He knew, of course, that he was in love with Bess-Istra. And he knew, of course, that she was in love with Stevens. How could she help but be? He wasn't so much of a boy as he had been. There was a new strength about him. If Bess-Istra had been changed by these astounding events, so had Stevens. He was a man, now. A man whom Bess-Istra loved.

The three of them listened in on the news constantly. Bandro now made a new edict that all power-gliders—and there were millions of them—would be equipped with a device that would make them controllable by the International Police. That is, any power-glider could be sent crashing to Earth by remote control at the will of any Scimitar!

Bill was grim. "The only way for anybody to travel for any great distance is by power-glider. All other vehicles have been scrapped. This means that if an army should get together, if there were ever any rebellion against Bandro's inhuman rule, his Scimitars could stop it—like that. The power-gliders carrying that army would be destroyed."

But inside, in the back of his mind, an idea was perking. He frowned. But he couldn't draw the thought out.

At the end of the month, every power-glider was equipped with the control device. And now Bandro made an announcement that filled Bill with the wild fire of hope. Bandro and Sab-Hallo were going to make a "good-will" tour of the world. They were going to stop off at various important cities and speak to the people. And they were going to make their tour in the spaceship that had originally brought them to this planet.

Bill snapped his fingers, whirled on Bess-Istra and Stevens.

"I've *got* it!" he yelled. "Bess-Istra—Johnny—I've got it! We're going to capture the spaceship..."

"Capture the—" Bess-Istra began blankly. Then her glorious, gold-flecked eyes glowed with savage lights.

"If we but could," she whispered. "Oh, Bill, if we could. But—"

The Reverend John Stevens shook his head gravely. "No, Bill." His glance was pitying. "We are only three against a world. Three against the entire International Police. We couldn't—"

"Listen!" Bill nearly shouted. "There are weapons on our power-glider which can cut through the hardest metals if they are applied closely enough, aren't there? We can cut through the hull of the spaceship, get inside, and play hell."

"But—"

"But nothing, Johnny. Don't you see? *We own the only power-glider in the world that cannot be controlled from a remote distance by the International Police.*"

AND the next day, the power-glider nosed out of the shrouding jungle with its human load. It hovered. But there was no sign that the Scimitars might still be looking for them. It was certain that Bandro thought them dead, their power-glider rusting away, sunk deep in jungle humus.

The glider shot high into the stratosphere. Bill turned its nose southwest. For a half-hour it bored at terrific speed. It was on the trail of the huge spaceship.

"*There it is!*"

There it was indeed. Miles below them, it plunged along at moderate pace through rolling heaps of storm clouds. It was far above land. It was on its way to San Francisco.

The power glider started to drop. Bill was tense at the controls. In a way this was utterly foolhardy. If the International Police—

"*Halt! Give your registration number. Immediately.*"

Bill's blood turned cold as the voice came from his *tele-radio.*

Spinning up toward them came a blunt-nosed Scimitar ship. It was a small ship. The three people could see two Scimitars inside.

Stevens whispered dully, "We'll have to give ourselves up."

"No." The word came from Bess-Istra. "Bill, this ship is the only one protecting the big ship. If we can—"

"Gotcha," Bill said huskily. "We'll try, anyway. Hang on!"

He touched the controls. The power-glider plunged headlong at the larger ship. Wind screamed.

"Stop immediately—*or you will be stopped!*"

Bill's heart was a stone in his breast. The ship had to get close enough. Could they make it?

They did!

The Scimitar ship, of course, depended on its remote control of the down-plunging power-glider. But this was the only power-glider in the world that couldn't be controlled in such a manner. And before the International Police realized that confusing truth, before they got over their surprise that the power-glider had not halted, those International Police were...*dead*.

Bill savagely sprayed the heat-ray over the transparent forepart of their ship. They burned.

At the last minute, Bill swerved the glider to escape collision. But it had been necessary to get as close as they could or else the heat-ray would have made the Scimitars only pleasantly warm. As it was, behind them the ship was a hurtling torch.

"Praise God," Stevens whispered, his voice shaking, from his prone position atop Bill. "In his infinite wisdom, the Lord knows that if we die, all hope dies. But now we shall live—shall see the world truly progress toward Utopia.

"But now we shall live..."

Bill was to remember those words.

Bess-Istra whispered joyously, "We have destroyed the spaceship's only protection. There is nothing to stop us, now. Downward, O Bill. Downward..."

And the power-glider dropped downward toward the broad black back of the great spaceship that held Bandro and Sab-Hallo; plunged through a rolling storm-cloud, and in almost complete blackness, landed.

CHAPTER FIFTEEN
Death of a Great Brain

BILL edged the glider along on the smooth surface until they came to a great round hatch.

"Play the heat beam there and fuse the clasp, and the hatch can be lifted," Bess-Istra whispered. "Hurry, Bill. Hurry!"

The heat-ray speared out. The hasp parted. And in another moment, working amid thunder and lightning, drenched to the skin with plummeting rain, the hatch swung up under Stevens' and Bill's labor.

Bess-Istra raised the glider, sent it silently through the dully-lighted aperture. Bill and Stevens dropped through the hatch to the lonely corridor below, pulling the hatch entrance down again.

"Tell me what I must do, O Bill..." Bess-Istra's voice sounded vibrantly. "And I will do anything if I can personally see to it that Sab-Hallo and Bandro get their just deserts."

Bill grinned to himself. Bess-Istra might have changed, but she wasn't a molly-coddle by any means.

He gave his instructions. Bess-Istra was to float along on the power-glider, close to the ceiling. Bill and Stevens would walk slightly in front, and try to detract attention from the glider. And at the propitious moment, Bess-Istra would blast whoever stood in their way toward the control room in the nose of the ship.

They started along. Bill's skin crawled. They were in the upper portions of a ship that swarmed with enemies, anyone of whom would kill them without mercy. To make it worse, neither Bill nor Stevens had a hand weapon.

Bess-Istra slanted the wings of the glider in toward the body of the ship as they padded down a well-lighted companionway. And just before they reached the bottom two officers of the great ship started up.

The officers looked upward at the two men, blinking. And the angle of their glance was such that they couldn't help but see the glider.

Bill's breath stopped. He halted in mid-step.

The leading officer cried something in his native language. His spastic-gun came out and up. In another moment, Bill and Stevens would have been doubled up in muscle-knotted slumber had not Bess-Istra acted. The heat-ray flashed out— and human flesh fried. The two Scimitar officers fell.

With one accord, the two men swooped down and took the spastic guns. Stevens' face was white, perspiring, but his lips were compressed.

"Way to go, Johnny," Bill spoke lowly. "Chin up. You'll see more dead bodies than this before it's over. Come on!"

And there were more dead bodies—a full score, before they finally reached the door of the control room.

But it was the only thing they could do, and they had to act quickly. Bill now drew a deep breath as the guard to the control room, whirled and died and fell; he let out his breath, jerked open the door, and stepped inside.

Bess-Istra and Stevens followed after him. And their presence was unknown until Bill cried ringingly, triumphantly...

"Stick 'em up, fellows. This is the big push—the blow-off! *Quick!*"

THERE were only three men in the control room. One was busily leaning over a map, another was at the controls, the third was at the cabinet of a *tele*-eye. This latter man was—Sab-Hallo!

The other two men turned before Sab-Hallo did. Sab-Hallo faced them slowly, like one who, even in defeat, tries to make a good entrance.

Sab-Hallo whispered, after a bitter moment, "And we thought you dead…"

He locked glances with Bess-Istra, his deadly hatred of her showing there. "You have ever stood in my way," he bit out. "I did your will only until I could step into your place. I did step into your place—"

"—but now shall step out," Bess-Istra flared. "You, whom I trusted and even now would wish to reinstate if—"

"Look out!"

The cry came from the Reverend John Stevens, a cry of horror.

Bill kept his muscles rigid, tried in a lightning-quick motion of his eyes to take in the whole scene. He saw the pilot of the ship, ignored up to now, draw a weapon. His evident intention was to kill Bess-Istra.

Bill moved his spastic-gun through a tiny arc, woodenly depressed the trigger. The spastic beams leaped out seizing the fellow's heart-muscle with invisible fingers, throttling it, causing it to stop its beat. The man fell.

Sab-Hallo screamed at that moment. His face contorted. He was like a broad-shouldered, squat gorilla as he leaped toward Bess-Istra, long arms outstretched. Bill did not have time to regain his balance. Bess-Istra was knocked backward to the floor, and the squat scientist, utterly maddened, ravened for her throat.

It was Stevens whose gun danced with tiny lights this time. The vibrations bathed the scientist's head, paralyzed his great brain. He rolled over, eyes staring upward sightlessly. For the brain, unconsciously, controls the life-mechanism of all parts of the body. Sab-Hallo was dead...

Bill scooped Bess-Istra to her feet. She immediately regained possession of her senses.

"The rest of the men in the ship!" she cried. "We must make sure—"

She darted for the control board of the great ship, lifted a panel, and depressed a stud.

"The sleep-gas!" she uttered triumphantly. "It will spread everywhere through the ship except to the control room. Oh, Bill—Johnny—we have won! The ship is ours. We can control it from this room, can go everywhere, invincible, impregnable, and shall seize all my disloyal men. Peace—real peace, this time—shall come to the planet Earth and shall endure.

Her eyes were glorified with her happiness, which was reflected in those of Stevens. And Bill himself understood the great thing that had happened. He felt a lump in his throat. The adventures they had gone through had been mad, *mad*. But it had all been for a purpose. They were here, the three of them who had seen so much of the great change— here, safe and alive!

There was no more danger, no more cause for alarm. It was hard to believe. But it was true. Sab-Hallo was dead. And their worst enemy, Bandro, was at this moment chained in slumber somewhere in the rest of the ship—

"Fools!" a voice grated. "So you thought to return, to take from me the reins of power."

The three people turned with varying degrees of speed to face Bandro!

BILL'S high hopes fell, like a boulder shoved over the brink of a sheer precipice; fell and splintered into a million pain-bringing shards.

He was held rooted, part of a tableau that existed for the better part of a minute.

Then Bess-Istra's voice, lifeless, weary, sounded: "We thought you to be in the other part of the ship—sleeping, helpless."

The world-tyrant laughed with mocking intonations.

"And so I would have been," he sneered, "had I not entered the control room while you were so busy with Sab-Hallo. I waited until an opportune moment—waited until you had convinced yourselves that you had succeeded in your purpose. And had you not been so busy with congratulating yourselves on a bold enterprise, it may have been that I would not have you at the point of a gun now."

"The moral being," Bill murmured numbly, "that you shouldn't cross your bridges before they're hatched. What's the pay-off?"

"Pay-off? Ah, yes. The pay-off is that you die."

Bill said, "As I suspected. So as the great hope of the world, we're complete flops, eh?" He laughed harshly, with a self-loathing that he did not bother to conceal. "Well, pal, if you insist on having fun, let's get it over with. I can't stand living with myself much longer."

He meant it. He had been in tough situations before. But always there had been some way out. Some slight chance of success. Here there was none. Bandro was too alert, too conscious of the fact that on the deaths of these three people rested all his hopes of future power. Bandro would not be caught napping. Nor was he going to waste any time in the vain, glorious braggadocio, which is usually the resort of the callow victor. He was going to sear them with destroying flame—now!

Bandro was holding two guns. Bill used to have trouble identifying the innumerable weapons these people from the stars had brought with them, but he recognized these as a particularly virulent type of heat-ray. Nope…not a chance.

Bandro's trigger fingers started to tense. Bill braced himself for momentary cutting agony, and in his last moments thought of Bess-Istra…

"Stay! In the name of the Lord our God, I command it!"

Bill's head whipped around toward Stevens so fast he almost jerked it loose.

"Johnny," he gasped. "For cryin' out loud, you can't—"

But the Reverend John Stevens, his eyes flashing fire, fearlessly stepped from the line and walked toward those guns that were just about to expel their deadly fires!

CHAPTER SIXTEEN
He Saved the World

BANDRO'S eyes bulged. He made a choking sound. He stiffened.

"And in the name of the Goddess Stuz, fool," he bit out, *"stay where you are!"*

The Reverend John Stevens stopped, but his head was held high. His voice was clear, his meaning plain.

"My God does not recognize the Goddess Stuz, unless she be Lucifer in disguise. And Stuz is helpless before Him, or before His servant."

Bill felt a shock of unbelief. For Bandro stood with slack jaw, sweat suddenly leaping to his face. His gun hand trembled visibly. Stevens took one more step forward, his expression serene, confident. Bandro stumbled back a step. A tremendous battle was evident on his face.

He cried in a tone of terrible wrath, "Move back—stop! I'll blast you!"

And:

"You dare not blast me," the young missionary replied. "The Lord will not permit us to die, when our mission is so great. *You will hand me your weapons.*"

Bill felt as if he were witnessing a miracle. Stevens might have been a saint, haloed, holding a radiant cross out before him, exorcising an evil spirit. For it was evident that Bandro was helplessly demoralized. Stevens was walking toward him, one hand outstretched to take the weapons. And Bandro was going to give them to him!

Or was he?

It almost worked.

But it didn't. At the last moment, the hypnotic spell in which Stevens held Bandro was dispersed. Perhaps the motion Stevens made toward the weapons was too sudden.

But Bandro fired.

Bill hardly knew what happened. He yelled. He plunged forward, saw Stevens fall, doubling up; but Bandro's attention could not be turned back to Bill fast enough to keep Bill from tangling with him.

Bandro's weapons went flying as Bill struck them from his hands. Bandro went bowling backward as Bill's fist connected with his chin. Went bowling backward, and smashed against the instrument panel of the great ship.

Bill caught a vague glimpse of Bess-Istra. She was looking with shocked glance at the heap of human flesh that was the Reverend Johnny Stevens. Then Bandro had rolled toward him again, face twisted in a scream of rage.

Bill smashed against a wall, was held spread-eagled there a moment. And in that moment, his blood froze.

IN THE vision screen above the instrument panel was the swiftly approaching Atlantic Ocean. Bandro's collision with the instrument board had changed the course of the great ship, and now it was plummeting at terrific speed toward the bosom of the broad sea below!

It was going to strike that heaving surface, was going to be immersed and rushing tons of water would flow through the hatch that Bill had opened.

Unless—Bill drew a deep breath, growled. He met Bandro's charge with the merciless purpose of a beast—to kill, and kill quickly. His fingers wrapped around Bandro's throat. He bore the man to the floor. Bandro's breath was hot on his face. Bandro's eyes bulged. Almost he succeeded in throwing Bill off. But Bill hung on, insensately, and finally dragged Bandro to his feet.

"Traitor!" Bill gritted.

He flung Bandro halfway across the control room. Bandro spun, twisted, smashed against the bulkhead, and sagged in a lifeless heap.

Bill stood over him, panting. But Bandro would never get up. Bandro's neck was broken. Bandro, tyrant of Earth, was dead.

Bill's head turned dazedly toward the vision screen. His brain awoke to life at last. The ship was so close to the ocean that Bill could see whitecaps.

In another second he was over the instrument board, panting, praying fervently. But he could make nothing of that hodge-podge of controls. It was hopeless. They were going to strike!

He whirled. "Bess-Istra!" he yelled. "The—"

But she was there, bending over the panel. She touched at buttons and finger-sized switches, her hands moving hurriedly. And just as the ship seemed certain to dip beneath the waves, Bess-Istra brought its nose up and sent it boring at a steep angle into the clouds.

In another minute, Bill was trembling with violent relief. The ship was sailing smoothly, controls locked.

Bess-Istra quickly turned from the instrument panel, with a numb expression. She stood over the Reverend John Stevens. Suddenly she crumpled up over him, and her racking sobs sounded through the ship.

Bill dropped to his knees, too, looking at the charred spot where a death-dealing ray had burned a hole through the missionary's head. Bill looked and couldn't believe it.

"Johnny," he said in a low, strained voice. "Johnny, you old son-of-a-gun. Wake up. It's all over. We've won. Sab-Hallo's dead. Bandro is dead. We've got a ship that nobody on Earth can stand up against. Everything that you wanted on Earth—peace and good will toward men, and so forth. Why, Johnny, we're just beginning, see? The war's over. There's no reason for you to die at a time like this. If it hadn't been for you we'd all be dead, and all hope would be dead—" He stopped, choking, eyes blurred.

Bess-Istra's head raised. She was blurred to Bill's sight.

"Say no more," she choked. "For Johnny is—oh, Bill, Johnny is no more... And he was so brave, and so true, and I loved him so."

BILL bowed his head. He bit at his lip. He said nothing. The Reverend John Stevens—like another—had sacrificed himself for humanity.

But finally he raised Bess-Istra's shaking body erect, drew her close against him while she sobbed out her grief—sobbed, not like a terrible woman from the stars, but like a girl of Earth whose heart is broken with pain unbearable.

Bill kept his eyes wide, his vision straight on the vision screen and the clouds through which the ship was sweeping. Well, it was all over now. All over. There were some loose ends to gather up; Bess-Istra would be made dictator of the world again because, after all, where could you get a better ruler? And Bill would report back to the New York Corey Features Syndicate and forever forget Bess-Istra.

Forget Bess-Istra? Oh, God, I don't want to forget her. I want her for myself—

"You loved him very much," Bill said gently.

"Because he was so good," she sobbed. "I loved him—as I would my own child, Bill—as I would a brother—"

Bill's arms tightened around her glorious body. He smiled. A great song of joy mingled with sadness beat in his pulses.

And she raised her swimming eyes to his, her lip trembling.

"Bill," she said huskily. "Bill. What—what do you think of me? Am I good...or am I bad? Am I never to be forgiven for the terrible things I did on that other world?"

Bill touched tenderly at her eyes, as if he could draw away the fright that showed there.

"Johnny Stevens would know the answer to that, Bess-Istra," he whispered. "Answer the question for yourself. Think back on what you've done on this world. You've stepped on a bunch of reptiles that didn't give a hoot for human life. Hitler, Tojo, Mussolini. Whatever you may have done in a past that is probably billions of years distant, it's nothing compared to the good that you've done here. Remember that, Mistress Bess; remember it always."

Her hands tightened on his shoulders. The fright was gone from her gold-flecked eyes. She breathed, "Yes, Bill. Yes...I will remember. And I will remember that there is so much to do before the people are completely happy—so much, Bill."

"Yes," he whispered huskily.

She did not answer. The tips of her fingers touched with infinite tenderness at the side of his face. A smile trembled on her perfect lips. In her moist eyes there was a light that Bill had vainly been hoping to see. He grew dizzy with the sight of it. He drew her lips to his and thrilled to her response; held her close and knew that she was his.

As the ship of peace thundered over a world that soon would go mad with joy at the release from all terrors, those two stood locked in close embrace, savoring the first ecstasy of a life that was to be rich indeed.

THE END

COME FLY WITH ME— AT THE SPEED OF LIGHT!

There was more to the maiden voyage of the Starling than just the ordinary test flight of another run-of-the-mill spacecraft. The Starling was the first of its kind—a spaceship built to travel at the speed of light.

Enthusiasm for the adventure that lay ahead was high. Scientist and pilot alike were bursting at the seams with impatience to see if their suped-up rocket ship would perform as hoped…

A simple test run…that was all it was supposed to be. But simple is not often the way Mistress Science behaves, and on that day she decided to serve up a wicked curve ball—a curve ball over the plate of the space-time continuum!

CAST OF CHARACTERS

CHARLES GILROY
The Starling was his baby, a spaceship like science had never seen before, but a simple test run got very unexpected results.

DAN BURDEEN
He was a world class space jockey, even if he was a little arrogant, overbearing, and blatantly abrasive.

PROFESSOR ALWARD
The real brains behind the Starling, he was a man ahead of his time—in more ways than one!

SUZANNE
She passed anxious hours waiting for her beloved's return from space…little did she know he'd actually been gone for months!

JULON
The leader of a dying planet—Earth! He discovered his people's future rested in the hands of two men from the past.

ELVAR
He was young, eager, and strong—and willing to risk his life on a journey into a land of degenerate beasts.

VARIS
It's not everyday a beautiful girl stuck on a cold, nearly dead planet runs into a man from the past who has the hots for her.

FLIGHT OF
THE
STARLING

By
CHESTER S. GEIER

ARMCHAIR FICTION
PO Box 4369, Medford, Oregon 97504

*For more information about Armchair Books and products, visit our
website at...*

www.armchairfiction.com

Or email us at...

armchairfiction@yahoo.com

CHAPTER ONE
The Hour Before Dawn

A TOUCH on my shoulder wakened me. I'd been sleeping lightly, troubled by uneasy dreams, and at the touch I was instantly alert.

The light in my room had been turned on. I found myself staring into the gaunt, angular features of Professor Alward, who was bending over my bed. A vague, instinctive fear, inspired by my dreams, vanished at the instant of recognition. Alward said:

"Time to get up, Charles. It'll be dawn soon." His eyes were dark-rimmed, his face pale and drawn. He had, apparently, sat up the entire night.

I nodded, swung aside the covers, and rose. Alward went to the door. He paused a moment, watching me somewhat anxiously. He still wore the oil-stained coverall in which I remembered seeing him, the day before, when we'd made the last delicate adjustments on the warp generators of the *Starling*, and his graying brown hair hung in disheveled locks over his forehead.

"You feel all right?" he asked.

"I feel fine," I said.

Alward smiled slightly, a little tiredly. "You and Dan are taking a considerable risk, you know, I have a terrible feeling of responsibility. I wouldn't like to have any further dangers added. The principle of the *Starling* looks all right on paper—but under actual operations, who knows what we may have overlooked?"

"I understand," I said. "I wouldn't be doing this if I weren't willing to accept the risks."

"It would help if I were able to go along..." Alward shrugged in leaden acceptance of the impossible. "I've already wakened Dan," he said. "You'll find breakfast waiting in the dining room," he nodded at me, and went out.

I began to dress. It was a more detailed process than usual, since I was not to wear ordinary clothes. My garments made up a typical spaceman's outfit. There was a long undersuit, a one-piece, zippered coverall of slate-gray plastolex, with a broad, flaring collar, fitting tightly at wrists and ankles, a pair of short boots with magnetic soles, a short, collarless jacket over which the coverall collar was to be folded, and a soft cap.

Splashing noises and snatches of discordant song came to me from Dan Burdeen's room next door. The blonde giant didn't seem at all concerned at what was to take place at dawn. As for myself, I was excited—and, I shall have to admit, not a little afraid. Our test flight in the *Starling* would be made under conditions that had never before been attempted by Man. And no one as yet knew fully the dangers attending space travel at speeds approaching that of light. The atomic engines of ordinary space vessels attained only a small fraction of the inconceivable velocity, which Alward claimed for the warp-drive of the *Starling*.

I WONDERED, with a sudden ache of anxiety, if Suzanne had anything to do with Burdeen's carefree mood. He'd spent most of the previous afternoon with her, while Alward and I finished our work on the ship. I'd caught a glimpse of them once, at the edge of the lake, talking earnestly. Had some decision, favorable to Burdeen, been made by Suzanne? I thought of this with a wrenching sensation almost like sickness.

I finished dressing, and went out into the hall. I caught sight of Burdeen at the head of the stairs, interrupted by my approach on his way down. He looked me over slowly, and grinned in the superior, taunting way I'd grown to know so well.

"Morning, runt," he said, pretending a great surprise. "So you didn't run away in the night after all, eh?"

Burdeen was six feet and some five inches tall, as handsome and perfectly proportioned as an ancient Greek statue. Considering the fact that I was just an ordinary six-footer, he felt that his advantage in height gave him the privilege to call me a runt.

I said, "Sorry to have disappointed you."

"You'll probably get cold feet and, back out yet," Burdeen said.

"Not before you do."

Burdeen eyed me levelly, almost grimly. "I never back out," he said, "of anything." And there was a quality in his voice and in his expression, which told me as clearly as words that he was referring not only to our coming flight but also to Suzanne.

I think Burdeen misunderstood my intentions regarding Alward's lovely niece, judging them on the basis of his own. I had known Suzanne for almost two years, since coming to work for Alward as his assistant. I hadn't, however, seen as much of her during that time as might have been expected. My work with Alward on the *Starling* had kept me busy the greater part of each day. Driven by the all-consuming fires of his great idea, Alward had permitted few interruptions.

Still, what I had seen of Suzanne convinced me that she was the only girl who would ever matter. Our occasional meetings and conversations were like fragments of a mosaic, meaningless in their individual selves, but making, when joined together, a complete and harmonious pattern. She drew me with the compelling attraction of one who has mutual interests, mutual understandings.

How much of my emotions for the grave, quiet girl were colored by compassion, I do not know. She had been orphaned as a child by the death of her parents in an air accident. And Alward, buried body and mind in his work, had proved a poor substitute. Existence for her had so far meant only a number of different schools and a parade of temporary companions. What she called home was a comfortless place, a sort of beehive of work and speculation over abstract things, which she could never quite grasp.

I had never spoken to Suzanne of my feelings. It had never occurred to me that she might even remotely care. I don't think I'd have known how to talk to her if I'd tried. My background was one of constant work and study. I'd never had a chance to develop any ingratiating social graces. In my relations with others, I felt a shyness and reserve, which I'd never been able to overcome.

Burdeen, on the other hand, didn't seem to be under any such handicap. Alward had hired him some two months before, to pilot the *Starling* on its test flight. Burdeen had promptly fallen in love with Suzanne—or at least developed an interest in her, which he interpreted as love. Such of his time as was not taken up by study of the operating principle of the ship and the handling of its controls, he spent in her company. I didn't know if Suzanne welcomed his attentions, though I wondered apprehensively at times.

BURDEEN was a typical spaceman, raw and hard, the product of a stern competitive world. He went after what he wanted with a contemptuous disregard for everyone else concerned. According to his code, the winner took all in a fight in which no holds were barred. My role was purely a passive one, but Burdeen chose to see in me a rival for the favor of Suzanne.

Burdeen sensed in my attitude that I'd caught his implied meaning. A derisive grin twisted his lips for an instant before he turned to continue on down the stairs. I followed slowly, conscious of a dull, listless anger.

Alward and Suzanne were seated at the table in the dining room, while Mrs. Svendt, the buxom housekeeper, bustled about with plates of steaming food. Burdeen and I took our places, amid a subdued exchange of greetings, and began to eat.

It was a tense and silent meal. Professor Alward, I noticed, did little more than play meaningless games with his food, his thin features drawn in a brooding frown. This was for him a crucial point in twelve years of almost constant work. I could understand his emotions. His life-long dream of building an interstellar vessel had, in the *Starling*, taken on material form; but whether or not the ship would prove a success remained yet to be seen. Failure, entailing the loss of twelve years and a sizeable fortune as well, couldn't have been easy for him to contemplate.

I glanced cautiously at Suzanne. Her dark head was bent over her plate, and what I could see of her small face looked troubled and withdrawn. She made an appealing picture of pensive loveliness. She wore a simple dress of dark green synthe-wool, and her hair was done up in the way I liked so well: parted in the center, swept back from the temples, and gathered in a mass of thick, tumbled curls at the nape of her neck. I knew, if she were to return my gaze, that her lashes and brows would be startlingly dark against the pale oval of her face, and that her eyes would be a very clear and disturbing hazel. But she didn't look in my direction.

I found myself wondering if her quietness indicated an anxiety for Burdeen, and possibly—just possibly—for myself. She could have no fears where Professor Alward was concerned, since he was not to accompany us on the test flight. His weak heart wouldn't have been able to bear the strains of acceleration.

An abrupt surge of hopelessness pulled my eyes from Suzanne. I felt a fool for thinking that she might be even slightly worried about me. If she were worried at all, it couldn't be over anyone but Burdeen. Seen through a woman's eyes, the tanned blonde giant, with his laughing blue eyes and carefree grin, was undoubtedly attractive. The very nature of his profession surrounded him with an aura of adventure and romance. Beside Burdeen, how could I have been noticed? I was just a glamorless physicist, scholarly, serious, and physically quite unimpressive.

Somehow or other, we got through the meal. I ate—but what I ate might have been just so much ashes for all the notice I paid it.

Alward sat back in his chair, and without any perceptible break in his musing, lighted his pipe. Suzanne glanced suddenly around the table, a little confused, as though she had forgotten where she was. She murmured an excuse, rose, and strode into the living room. With a grin of delight, Burdeen rose hastily to follow her.

ALWARD and I were alone. I lighted a cigarette and puffed at it abstractedly, thinking of dawn and of Suzanne. After a while, Alward spoke.

"Charles."

"Yes?" I said, jerking my reluctant mind back to reality.

"Everything's all right, isn't it?"

"I'm sure everything is all right, sir. Our check-up yesterday was thorough enough."

Alward passed a hand wearily over his face. He said slowly, "I've thought of this moment for years. I was sure I had everything all planned out, beyond the faintest possibility of error. And now...I'm not sure. Now that the actual test is to begin, I feel that I created something too big for understanding or certainty."

"You're tired, sir," I said. "The ship will work."

"You understand everything you are to do?"

I nodded. Alward pulled reflectively at his pipe for some seconds. Then he said:

"It's almost dawn. I've thought of a slight change in course which I'd like to discuss with Dan before you leave." Some of Alward's old energy seemed to flow back into him. He rose and went to the living room entrance. I heard him call Burdeen.

Burdeen's voice answered, and Alward explained his idea. Burdeen's tone grew a trifle sharp.

"That will have to be put on the flight charts—and they're all in the hangar."

"We'll go there, then. It's almost time to leave anyway."

Alward turned and strode from the room, obviously on his way to the hangar. After a moment, Burdeen followed, visibly annoyed. It was tacitly understood that I was to accompany them, but for some obscure yet irresistible reason, I hung back. I heard the measured thuds of their feet on the porch outside, and then, faintly, the scrape of their soles on the gravel path which led to the hangar. Then there was silence.

I knew suddenly why I had remained behind. I turned slowly back to face the living room entrance, thinking abruptly, achingly, of Suzanne. And as though in answer to my thoughts, the figure of the girl appeared without warning in the entrance.

I stared at her—guiltily. Her hazel eyes widened on my face, and one small hand crept to her throat. We gazed at each other for a long moment, with a lack of sound or motion that was oddly unreal, dreamlike. Finally Suzanne said:

"Why, Charles, I thought you had gone."

"I...I just wanted to say good-bye."

"But you'll be back, won't you?"

"...Yes." I looked away, with an embarrassed feeling, as though I'd just done something foolish.

There was a rustle of motion, and suddenly I felt Suzanne's hands on my arms. The delicate oval of her face seemed dilated with fear.

"Charles—you don't think there's a chance that...that you might not come back?"

"We'll be back. Dan will come back. There's really no danger."

Her fingers tightened momentarily on my arms. "Oh, Charles! I wasn't thinking of Dan." She sounded impatient, almost angry. But she looked as if she wanted to cry.

I gazed stupidly down at her, pondering a little bewilderedly the implication of her words. Then I understood. And then suddenly, somehow, she was in my arms and my cheek was pressed tightly against her hair, and a kind of roaring silence beat over me and through me in great, slow waves.

After a while I looked at her and said, "But Dan?"

"Forget Dan," she said.

"I...I must seem terribly dumb. I never guessed— But I love you, Suzanne. Did you know?"

She shook her head, hazel eyes smiling at me through tears. "I didn't know. I only knew that you were serious and kind...the way my father must have been."

"And you love me?"

"Of course."

She was in my arms again. I don't know how long we stood there when I realized that the darkness beyond the encircling windows had grown gray with approaching light.

It was dawn.

CHAPTER TWO
The Flight

WE WALKED slowly, Suzanne and I, down the steps of the porch, to the gravel path, which led to the hangar. A few faint streaks of rose and gold showed already in the brightening sky to the east. There was the moist, fresh smell of morning in the air, and the surrounding trees loomed vaguely ghost-like in a gray haze. A cold, thin breeze drifted from the dark expanse of the lake.

It was quiet, with the deep quiet of open spaces that I'd grown to love. The house and its grounds were located in a wilderness of trees and hills. They had once been the site of a vacation resort, abandoned when spending vacations in space or on the Moon had become the fad. Considering Alward's desire for secrecy, the spot had been ideal in which to work. Except for the hangar, sheltering the completed *Starling*, he had made few additions or changes.

Suzanne stopped, gazing out over the lake. Her voice came to me after a moment, low and faintly bitter.

"It happened—but so late. Why didn't we make it happen before?"

"It happened anyway, Suzanne."

"I'm thinking of the flight, Charles. I'm afraid."

"There's nothing to be afraid of. The ship will work. I helped build it. I understand it. I know it will work."

She swung around to face me. "You'll come back?"

"I'll come back, Suzanne. I won't let anything stop me."

"I'll be waiting…"

I took her in my arms and held her tightly a moment. Then I released her slowly and said:

"I have to go."

"Yes," she said. "You have to go."

The hangar lights had been turned on. Alward and Burdeen stood near the open entrance port of the *Starling*. They had obviously just finished their discussion.

Burdeen's blue gaze narrowed slightly as he saw me with Suzanne. Then he grinned as though dismissing it as insignificant, and strode forward. He spoke to Suzanne, ignoring me.

"I'm glad you came. You're just in time to see us off."

Suzanne nodded gravely. "Goodbye, Dan. And good luck." She made no move of invitation, but Burdeen bent suddenly and kissed her.

I said nothing. For the first time since I'd known him, I felt a little sorry for Burdeen.

Suzanne turned to me, touching my arm. "Good-bye, Charles," her eyes told me that our previous farewell, beyond the need for any further demonstrations, was a secret we would share.

I said, "Good-bye, Suzanne." Then Burdeen and I shook Alward's hand and waited while he and the girl walked back to the house. It wouldn't have been safe for them to remain in the hangar when the ship took off.

Finally they were gone. Burdeen continued to gaze after them, frowning, as though something was puzzling him.

I turned to look at the slim, tapering shape of the *Starling*, gleaming silver-gray under the hangar lights. It had once been an ordinary atomic rocket, a private cruiser model just coming into general use. Alward and I had removed the protruding jet tubes, useless for our purposes, and now its metallic skin stretched sleek and unbroken. Interior changes had also been made. Alward's atomic power driven warp-generators had been substituted for the original atomic engines, and the plan of cabins and passageways had been altered to fit in the new machinery. The ship was just a mere shell of its former self. In the pursuit of our work, Alward and I had stripped it ruthlessly of nonessentials. We had not bothered afterward to restore fully its previous comforts and luxuries. Since the first flight was to be a short one, few of these were needed anyway.

AS I looked at the ship, a surge of excitement rushed over me with the thought that Burdeen and I stood at last upon the threshold of our adventure. For it was an adventure, as are essentially the steps into the unknown, with their accompanying dangers, taken by all pioneers. We would be the first men in history to travel at a speed close to that of light itself. If we returned, we would see, as a result of the risks we had taken, the dawn of a new era—the era of interstellar travel. That alone outweighed beyond consideration the value we placed upon our respective lives.

The circumstances of the flight itself were simple. We were to circumnavigate the Sun—or at least insofar as following a vast elliptical orbit can be called circumnavigation. It would take some three hours. Only a half-hour of this time would be spent traveling close to light speed. The rest would be consumed in accelerating and decelerating. It would not be an easy flight, since for the greater part of the time Burdeen and I would be subjected to terrific pressures, which our special cushioning seats, with their tremendously powerfully absorbing springs, would alleviate but not entirely nullify.

I became abruptly aware that Burdeen had turned and was watching me. His blue eyes seemed oddly intent, speculative. He studied me a moment longer, then said:

"Well, runt, are you getting in—or have you finally decided to back out?"

"I'd be the last one in the world to provide you with an excuse to back out yourself," I said. I climbed into the ship and made my way to the control room. I was seated in my chair, fastening the wide, thick safety straps, when Burdeen entered.

He dropped into his chair and fumbled for his safety straps. He looked thoughtful. He didn't buckle them about his body immediately, but held them absently, glancing at me. Something was on his mind.

Burdeen said finally, "You're acting pretty cocky, runt."

Anger was a sudden glow inside me. But I managed to speak quietly when I answered.

"Burdeen, this is no time for personalities. We've got a job to do—a job that's bigger than either of us. We aren't going to get it done by airing our spites."

He ignored me. "Listen, runt, I want to know something. Is there anything between you and Suzanne?"

The glow inside me became a hot blaze of fury. "You're damned right there is," I said. "Suzanne loves me. And now, if you have any sense at all, you'll forget about her and start flying this ship."

In a flash of motion, Burdeen leaped out of his chair, and his big fingers closed like the jaws of a steel trap on the front of my jacket.

"You're a liar!" he said. "You're a rotten liar!" His voice was thick, choking.

"You know better than that," I answered evenly. "It's either you or I, if anyone, that Suzanne cares about. And you know very well she hasn't anything for you, but you aren't willing to admit it—not even to yourself."

I was unable to move. It was the safety straps, however, rather than Burdeen's grip which held me powerless. I think he realized this after a moment. He released me with a disdaining jerk of his arm. He said grimly:

"I'm going to have this out with Suzanne. We're going to settle this once and for all."

"You'll succeed only in making a fool of yourself," I told him. "Besides, the flight is the only important thing right now. We've delayed long enough."

BURDEEN slowly grew calm. A mask seemed to slide over his face. He dropped back into his chair and completed his initial act of fastening his safety straps. Then he turned his attention to the controls.

It was a truce, an armed truce that would exist until we returned. But remembering Burdeen's secretive expression, I wondered suddenly if he didn't have other plans. I knew he wasn't the sort to give up easily. He wanted Suzanne. I was in the way. And if an "accident" happened to me while we were in space, who would be the wiser? It didn't seem at all a far-fetched idea. I knew the way Burdeen's mind worked.

Further uneasy speculation in this direction was blotted out as I heard the soft hum of the warp generators. The hum deepened. The *Starling* began to move. Easily, gently, it lifted from the floor of the hangar, and at Burdeen's touch on the controls, floated through the doorway into the dawn outside. In the view-plate, tiny but perfect in detail, I saw before the house the figures of Alward and Suzanne. They stared a moment, motionless, as though surprised that the ship had moved. Then they began waving excitedly.

The hum deepened still more, became something felt rather than heard. The scene in the view-plate tilted crazily as Burdeen pointed the nose of the ship toward space. Then in a flash of motion, the trees and hills, and then the green and brown of the land, vanished. There was just the blue of the sky around us, deep and limitless. We were on our way.

On the forward control panel the chronometer ticked off the first few minutes of our epochal flight. The hum of the generators filled the silence like the vast, deep roar of a distant river. We were riding the warp, hurtling through the atmospheric envelope at an ever-increasing velocity.

I must explain at this point how the ship worked. Greatly limited by the nature of the subject, it cannot be—nor do I intend it to be—a very accurate or illuminating explanation. Only mathematics can give the ultimate, clear picture of Alward's tremendous conception.

Driven by atomic energy, the generators created a force as the generators of the past created electricity. In some respects the force *was* electricity, but it was of a higher energy order, containing inherent magnetic properties in a complete union of a kind only vaguely suggested by the term "electro-magnetic," in which the two forces involved are more or less mutually exclusive, the one giving rise to the other. The force created in the immediate vicinity of the ship a warp in space—a moving warp, which could with fair accuracy be called a ripple in the fabric of space. The ship rode this moving warp or ripple as a surfboard rides the moving crest of a wave. The intensity of the force controlled the speed of the warp up to a certain limit.

This is where the full import of Alward's principle enters in. The velocity of light through space is a constant set by the very nature of space itself, in exactly the same manner that the velocity of light through air, glass, or water may be said to be a constant set respectively by the nature of these materials. The velocity of light through space, therefore, is the ultimate velocity at which any object—tenuous as light, or solid as a ship—can travel through space. Although, in theory, the propelling power of the force was unlimited, we would not, because of this factor, exceed the speed of light. Nor were we, in actual practice, even to attain it, since the solidity of the ship, in contrast with the tenuity of light, would produce a kind of friction with space that would hold us considerably under light speed. The fact still remained, of course, that we would travel faster than Man had ever traveled before, or ever would travel—in this space.

AS THE acceleration of the *Starling* increased, a giant hand seemed to touch and then to press slowly and inexorably upon my body. The sky, as seen in the view-plate, gradually turned a deep, dark blue. Then it was purple, shading slowly to black, and the stars began to blaze in their full, unobscured magnificence.

Burdeen, reclining in his huge chair, seemed almost at ease, except that his features were set and tense, his eyes darting from the various dials, gauges, and indicators on the control panels to the studs and switches set in the arm of his chair and manipulated by his fingers. Though I could have piloted the ship in an emergency—my purpose in being aboard—I could not but admire him a little now that he was at work. I could overlook for a moment the unpleasantness between us and see him objectively as he was—a pilot, and a good one. Even at controls different from those to which he was accustomed, his touch was deft and sure.

In what seemed only a short time, we were beyond the atmosphere of Earth and in space. There was no color in the view-plate now. There was only the incredibly deep, soft, utter blackness of the void, strewn and dotted with countless intolerably brilliant pinpoints of light.

With the difficulty under the pressing weight of acceleration, I reached a hand to the controls in the arm of my chair, dual with Burdeen's, and turned the dial, which would change the scene in the view-plate. The Earth appeared a tremendous orb, bluish-green and misty with silvery atmospheric haze. It grew visibly smaller as the minutes passed, seeming to shrink in upon itself, and became a great disc that dwindled more and more rapidly. We were already going very fast—faster than any atomic rocket had ever gone—and our speed was still increasing.

The giant's hand of acceleration was pushing me deep into the immensely thick padding of my chair. The absorbing springs were taking most of the relentless pressure, but my body seemed still a weight of tons. I had a trapped, impotent, smothered feeling. How long, I began to wonder anxiously, would it go on? How long could flesh and bone hold out? Would it turn out that our goal of speed was a thing impossible for mere, weak humans to attain?

A fog crept over my eyes, a gray fog tinted with a red haze of pain, and a blackness and numbness began to fill the corners of my mind. I was losing consciousness. But with the faculties still in my grasp, I wondered apprehensively about Burdeen. If he passed out, the ship, unguided, might very well plunge into the Sun, or stray so far into the uncharted vastness of space as to become hopelessly lost.

Burdeen didn't pass out, however, as I learned later. There was a giant's resistance in that giant body of his. And he was, after all, more accustomed to the ordeals of acceleration than myself.

As it developed, I didn't lose consciousness entirely. I managed somehow to keep a kind of fingernail grip on my awareness of things. There were periods which I do not recall clearly, when I seemed to be floating alone in a star-shot darkness with a troubling impression of material things around me, of instruments and machines. It was a kind of semi-state experience on the borderline between sleep and waking.

I DON'T know how much time passed when I gradually became more cognizant of my surroundings. The unutterable, terrific pressure on my body seemed slowly to be easing. And then came the interval when I was fully alert.

The pressure slowly lifted, and by degrees a sensation almost of comfort stole over me. I soon found that I could move without difficulty.

I glanced at Burdeen. His face was pale, his eyes sunken and blood-shot. Yet there was an air of indomitable energy about him. He had been shaken, but not bowed.

He returned my gaze after a moment. He smiled thinly and spoke, his voice a mere whisper of sound.

"This is it! We're doing it!"

"We're approaching light speed?"

"Yes. One hundred and eighty-six thousand miles a second now. Think of it, runt—one-hundred and eighty-six thousand miles a second!" There was awe and exultation in Burdeen's tone.

As we reached our maximum, constant speed, all sense of pressure finally vanished. I was exhausted, with a feeling of soreness in every fiber, but aside from this, my sensations were those ordinarily experienced during free flight in space. There was little indication of our incredible velocity. The stars in the view-plate, to each side of us remained visually much the same. Those immediately in front of us, however, showed a noticeable Doppler effect. The Earth was a bright green star far to our rear, and the Sun was an intolerable ball of incandescence off our port side. For very obvious reasons, I didn't attempt a look at the Sun, or otherwise use it as a means of reference.

A little over an hour and a half had passed. The chronometer continued busily to tick off the seconds. It seemed fantastic, even while I knew it was true, to think that each tick of the chronometer measured off a span of over one-hundred and eighty-six thousand miles.

Time passed more slowly as the unbelievable was accepted, digested, and rendered commonplace. Burdeen and I said nothing to each other. He was pressing forward against his safety straps, glancing from the instruments to the view-plate, features intent and hawkish. I was not a little tense myself, everything seemed to be turning out all right. But would it last?

Minutes that were centuries of nervous strain dragged by. Finally Burdeen reached once more for the controls in the arm of his chair. The crucial, all-important half-hour had past—and safely. We would now begin decelerating for the return to Earth. It was a delicate task. Instead of riding the warp, we would now be using it to slow our speed, in somewhat the same way that a gradually applied brake slows a spinning wheel.

MY EXHAUSTION pulled at me like an insistent hand. I didn't try to resist it. I slumped back into my chair, as far as my safety straps would let me, and closed my eyes. I'd seen everything there was to see on the trip out. And having traveled close to light speed had dulled my interest in further wonders.

I think I slept. The next thing I knew, Burdeen had me by the arm and was shaking me roughly.

"Gilroy! Wake up! Something has happened!" In his excitement, he forgot to call me runt.

I stared at him, struggling for full alertness, and asked, "What's the matter?"

"The Earth! Look at it."

I turned my eyes in sudden apprehension to the view-plate. The immense bluish-green orb of Earth filled the entire screen. I gazed at it for a moment, perplexed. Nothing seemed to be wrong. It was Earth as it would normally be upon our return.

Then I understood. It was Earth, true enough—but somehow not the same Earth that we had left some three hours previously.

The continents of North and South America were in our field of vision. They were still recognizable, still much the same to casual scrutiny. But a moment's study showed that they had changed. The shapes of the two continents were not the same as I had last seen them. It was as though the oceans had risen, or the land had sunk in spots. And snow covered great areas of their surfaces. The colors were now predominantly white and greenish-brown instead of the brown and green that I remembered.

A thought rose above the clouds of dazed horror, which filled my mind. I reached for the view-plate dial, tense with dread at what I might see.

Under my fingers, the scene changed. Space and its countless blazing stars appeared. I stared at them numbly.

I couldn't recognize a single star. The old, familiar constellations were gone. Stars still formed patterns and designs across the ebon background of space, singly and in groups—but none that I knew. The constellations in the view-plate were different, strange—alien.

I reached for the dial again, turned it slowly. But when the disc of the Sun came into view, it wasn't necessary to shield my eyes. The Sun was a shrunken reddish orb. It looked tired and worn, a little unhappy.

I looked slowly at Burdeen. In his blue eyes was the same question that must have been mirrored in my own.

What had happened to the world and the cosmos we knew?

CHAPTER THREE
Valley of the Machines

THERE was a long silence, while dismay faded slowly from our minds and the fun scope of the mystery to which we had returned began to penetrate. Finally my attention focused once more on the view-plate, and I brought Earth—or what we had known as Earth—back in its field. I think I had the dim hope that a second look would somehow find everything normal. But I was doomed to disappointment.

Burdeen said, "Gilroy...you're a scientist. What do you think caused this?"

"I couldn't say for certain just yet," I told him. "I haven't anything to go on. But a good guess would be that it was brought about in some way by traveling close to light speed."

Burdeen looked at the image in the view-plate, and then at me. "I've been thinking about it, Gilroy. Maybe...maybe that isn't the Earth at all. Maybe traveling close to light speed threw us out of our own Universe entirely."

"I don't know," I said. "The planet looks a lot like Earth. And if there's a moon..."

"There is," Burdeen said. "I saw it as we circled in."

"Then it must be Earth."

"But the changes—the snow, the stars, the sun...?"

"I don't know," I said again.

There was a silence. After a while Burdeen gestured helplessly and asked:

"Well, what are we going to do? This wasn't in the instructions Alward gave me."

"We might as well do what we intended to do upon our return—land." I shrugged listlessly. "There's no other place to go."

"How about the house—the spot where we took off?"

"We wouldn't be able to find it. Look at the view-plate. The landmarks, which were to have guided us back to the house, are gone. There's only snow down there—snow and ice. The house is gone, too." I thought abruptly, piercingly, of Suzanne. She had gone with everything else.

Burdeen straightened with returning purpose. "There ought to be people down there somewhere," he said, turning to the controls. "If we can find them, they might be able to help us."

I clutched at the thought. Alward had had the foresight to load aboard a store of emergency provisions. These wouldn't last forever. People meant food and shelter. But *what*, I wondered, if there *were* no people?

The ship sped toward the planet at gradually decreasing speed. Burdeen made adjustments on the controls from time to time. Soon the immense sphere was no longer convex, but concave, and its continents began to fill the entire field of vision. We dropped down toward the middle of what had once been North America—or what appeared to resemble it.

Finally we were within a thousand feet or so over the surface and moving eastward. We watched the view-plate eagerly. But no roads or buildings showed below us. There was only the snow, interspersed with glittering patches of ice, and great forests of what appeared to be firs and pines. The country had all the characteristics, which the far North had once shown.

Presently we reached a great city. It didn't seem, from its location, to be Chicago. The city was like no city I had ever known. It was an incredible, sprawling maze of colossal towers, strung level upon level with leaping spans. The towers gleamed metallically in the pale, cold light, unmarred by the storms of countless years.

WE CRUISED slowly over the city for a while, searching for signs of life. But there were none that we could see. From the highest spans, down to the lowest visible levels, nothing moved. The glittering mantle of snow which layover the city was everywhere smooth and unbroken.

Burdeen said slowly, "It's deserted. Everybody's gone."

"There should be other cities," I said. "They can't all be deserted."

"Where? Further north?"

"No, it's cold there. If any people remain, they would most logically inhabit the warmer, southern regions." Burdeen nodded, and turned back to the controls. The ship swung around, and soared in the general direction of the Gulf of Mexico. Near the coast, we turned west. Our speed was slowed, and we moved some five hundred feet above the surface.

The snow was thinner here than toward the north. It covered the ground only in occasional patches. Trees here were profuse in numbers and in variety, and grasses and shrubs carpeted great expanses of the land. But an atmosphere of desertion lay heavy over everything. It was as though we moved over a wilderness where the feet of Man had never trod. There were no roads. The few houses we saw were so apparently neglected that we knew people no longer lived in them.

Our discouragement grew as time passed. We were about ready to stop the search when the ship moved over a great rectangular valley. Almost at once we saw the buildings scattered over its floor. The buildings were rather widely scattered, except at one point, approximately in the valley's center, where they were numerous enough to form what seemed to be a small city. The ground bordering the city and between the scattered buildings showed the patchwork effect of soil under cultivation. As we descended for a closer inspection, we saw in the tilled fields glinting, angular shapes that clearly were farming machines. They were in motion, performing obscure tasks among the crops. They seemed to be working without human guidance, for we saw no men anywhere near them.

Burdeen flashed me a grin of joy and relief. I nodded my understanding. Farms and farming machines indicated the presence of people. The valley was inhabited.

Moving very slowly now, we drew over the city. It was very small, more like a town or village, its buildings laid out in a neat geometric pattern. The buildings were white and small, with the classical simplicity of ancient Grecian architecture. The ground between them was arranged and tended with the order and care of a park or garden. Scattered about were what seemed to be numerous statues and fountains. And there were people. They stood about in groups, staring up at the ship in surprise. As we watched, more came running from the buildings—and others floating through the air. Burdeen and I were startled until we realized that the floating figures had flying apparatus of some sort strapped to their shoulders.

Burdeen glanced at me. "Looks as if it'll be all right to land."

I nodded agreement. "These people are civilized. It isn't likely that they'll make trouble." I realized, suddenly, without feeling much surprise over the fact that relations between Burdeen and myself were friendlier than at any time since we'd met. It was understandable enough. We shared a common problem. We, each to the other, were the only familiar things in a world where all else had changed. The spites and quarrels of the past had been paled into insignificance by the perplexities and dangers of the present.

Burdeen set the ship down on a broad expanse of lawn before a building that might have been a temple lifted bodily from ancient Athens. Thus ended—or seemed to end at the time—the *Starling's* incredible flight. A little less than eight hours had passed.

Burdeen began to unbuckle his safety straps. "We'll go out and talk to them," he said. "Maybe they can tell us where we are."

WE WERE both very stiff from the long confinement to our chairs, and had to spend a few minutes in limbering up. Then, straightening his jacket and setting his cap at a rakish angle over his blonde hair, Burdeen strode toward the entrance port. I followed after him with turbulent feelings, the most predominating of which seemed to be excitement.

Together, Burdeen and I unsealed the port and pushed it open. The people had gathered in a crowd before the ship. As the port swung out, revealing us, they drew back, abruptly silent. Amid a deep quiet, Burdeen and I climbed down from the port and to the ground.

I gazed at the nearest of the figures with the same curiosity with which they were staring at me. Oddly enough, the very first impression I received made me think of Burdeen's runt epithet. Applied to me here the term would no longer be one of spite, but of literal accuracy. For the people were all fully as tall, or taller, than Burdeen. The similarity didn't end there, since the majority had blonde hair and a statue-like perfection of features and form. And so many of the staring eyes were blue, that I began to have somewhat the feelings of a stranger at a family reunion. I think I lost at that moment a lot of my incipient friendliness for Burdeen.

The people were simply yet colorfully dressed. They wore long-sleeved tunics, belted at the waist, and falling mid-way to the knees. Their feet were covered with a kind of light boot, which molded snugly to ankles and calves. Over their tunics they wore voluminous, hooded cloaks, or belted, short coats, also hooded. The wearers of this latter type of garment seemed to be those Burdeen and I had glimpsed flying through the air, for crisscrossing straps bound an apparatus of some sort to their shoulders.

The air was cool without being actually cold, and it had the crisp tang which only early morning or autumn air seems to have. A light but steady breeze touched my face, laden with the fresh, clean smell of grass. I could hear the musical gurgling of a nearby fountain, and from somewhere overhead came a flutter of wings from curiously circling birds, with occasional inquiring twitters or trills.

Abruptly, a new sound came. It was that of a voice, a deep, authoritative voice, raised in a tone of command. A ripple of motion spread through the crowd. The massed figures before Burdeen and myself parted, and a man strode with vigorous self-assurance into the intervening space and came toward us.

He was an old man, but as straight and purposeful as, a youth of half his years. He was dressed much like the others, except that his tunic, partly visible through the opening in his cloak, fell to his ankles and a silver chain bearing a medal or badge hung from his neck. The hair beneath his hood was long and white, and his features were finely patrician, grave with the responsibilities of leadership, but without any of its arrogance of stiffness. From blue eyes piercing beneath the snowdrift overhang of white brows, he surveyed first Burdeen and me, and then the gleaming shape of the *Starling* behind us.

A murmur rose from the crowd. I could not distinguish what was said, but one word seemed frequently to be repeated. It was "Julon"—obviously the name of the patriarch who stood before me. And as though the crowd drew courage and confidence from his presence, the murmurs swelled and deepened.

Julon half turned, and his peremptorily lifted hand brought immediate silence. Then he faced Burdeen and me once more. He spoke. What he said was put in the form of a question, but I didn't understand the words. They seemed vaguely familiar, in the way that words in the English of Chaucer would have been familiar, but without essential meaning.

Burdeen glanced at me, his features puzzled. I shook my head to show that my understanding of Julon's question was little better than his own.

JULON seemed to realize that his language was strange to us. He considered a moment, brows furrowed in thought, evidently pondering his next move. Finally he pointed from Burdeen and me to the ship, and waved a hand at the sky.

"He probably wants to know if we came from some place a great distance away," I told Burdeen.

"I guess that can be answered in the affirmative," Burden said. "It's true enough," he turned to Julon and nodded emphatically, waving his own hand at the sky.

Julon seemed satisfied. Turning to the grouped people behind him, he spoke a few words of explanation. A stir of excitement ran through the gathering. Voices rose in sudden, eager babble.

Julon attempted a few more questions in sign talk, but the ideas behind them this time were a bit too complex to grasp. He seemed to want to know our purpose in coming to the valley. It would have been too difficult to explain, if that actually was the gist of his inquiries. How could Burdeen and I have made him understand that we had landed in the valley with the vague, desperate hope of finding some way to return to the world we had originally left?

With a smile of resignation, Julon abandoned his efforts. He dismissed the crowd with a few quiet words of command, then indicated that Burdeen and I were to accompany him.

For the first time, I noticed that Julon had a companion, a stalwart, golden-haired young giant who was a younger edition of himself, and apparently his son. Julon laid a hand on the shoulder of the youth and said: "Elvar." It was obviously an introduction.

I smiled and nodded. Pointing to myself, I said: "Charles Gilroy."

Burdeen spoke his own name, his glance at Elvar faintly challenging. They were of a size, and except for a certain classical refinement in Elvar's features, they might easily have been mistaken for brothers. Elvar grinned a trifle self-consciously, acknowledging the introductions with a bow.

Gesturing, Julon finally turned and began to walk briskly toward some point in the spacious, garden-like city. Burdeen and I hesitated only long enough to close and lock the entrance port of the *Starling,* then turned to follow him.

Little groups of people stood everywhere. They fell silent as we passed, glancing at us curiously. They seemed entirely friendly and no more inquisitive than any other people would have been under the same circumstances, but there seemed to be a restrained eagerness about them that puzzled me. The arrival of Burdeen and myself in the valley seemed to mean something to them.

Flying figures passed over us frequently as we strode along. And complex machines of all sizes and shapes, and as far as I could see, uncontrolled, sped smoothly over the grass, bound on mysterious errands. They seemed intelligent in ways I had never guessed a machine could be. A few times, when our progress blocked the path of one, it detoured carefully around us, as though aware of us not merely as obstructions, but as human beings. The machines and the flying figures were oddly jarring notes against the classical atmosphere of the city.

CHAPTER FOUR
Revelations

WE CAME at last to a small single-storied white house that resembled a temple of some minor deity in ancient

Greece. On the steps before the house stood two women. They had apparently been attracted outdoors by the hubbub of the *Starling's* arrival. Both were fully as tall as I, a fact that did little to bolster my already tottering morale.

Introductions were performed again. By means of Julon's sign talk, interspersed with a few spoken words, I learned that the women were Mera and Varis, respectively Julon's wife and daughter. Mera was a kind-faced, matronly woman, with a poised, erect bearing, which I can describe only as queenly. And Varis...she was too beautiful to be entirely real. She was a vision of flowing golden hair, sea-blue eyes, and gleaming white skin. But even at first glance it was evident that she was no mere exterior shell of feminine perfection. There was flame and spirit in her, and a quick, all-embracing intelligence.

Burdeen stared at Varis with the startled incredulity of one who sees, but is reluctant to believe. She flushed under the intensity of his gaze and looked away. As for myself, I could see in her bright beauty only the grave, dark loveliness of Suzanne—lost to me across the mysterious gulf, which the voyage near light speed had placed between us. Thought of Suzanne filled me with a sudden, aching desolation. It didn't seem possible that I would ever see her again.

Julon chuckled tolerantly at Burdeen's fascinated expression and gestured toward the doorway. We strode into the house. The interior was simply, yet comfortably furnished. Deep rugs covered the floors. Large globes hanging from the ceilings shed a clear, steady light on marble walls, broken in places by niches containing statuettes and vases, or hung with rich tapestries that glittered metallically. Scattered about were tables and couches, all exquisitely carven and inlaid.

Elvar took Burdeen and me to a room at one side of the house, obviously a kind of sleeping chamber, for the couches here were deep and broad, resembling beds. We took turns in washing in streams of hot and cold water which flowed from opposite sides of a niche in one wall into a deep basin set at waist level. Drying ourselves on thick, soft towels, we followed Elvar to another room, filled with the savory odor of cooked food.

Presently Julon, Mera, and Varis appeared, and the meal began. It was very much like the buffet suppers I had attended once. Each helped himself to food set out on trays before a broad, high cabinet of glass and metal, then sat down on the couches about the room to eat from the plate which he held on his knees. The cabinet was a highly complex cooking device of some sort. Low bubbling, hissing, and humming sounds drifted from it, and by means almost like magic, it removed used trays of food and set out new ones. I learned later that it prepared and cooked the food entirely by itself, needing only a few spoken directions as to variety and amount. It was kept supplied by still other machines.

The food had an exotic flavor, but it was delicious and satisfying, essentially like the food I've always eaten. Just then, however, I was too hungry to be critical—or very careful about my manners, though the meal was informal enough.

WHEN we had finished, Julon beckoned us to a room which Burdeen and I had seen when first entering the house. It seemed to be the living room. Following the example of the others, we settled ourselves upon one of the couches and waited expectantly for what was to happen next. There was an unmistakable deliberate air about the proceedings.

Julon strode to a tapestry on the wall and pulled it aside. A large screen was revealed, with an operating mechanism below it, set in the wall. The screen looked much like a television or view-plate screen, but as I was shortly to learn, it didn't quite serve the same purpose.

From a receptacle near the operating mechanism, Julon produced what seemed to be a spool of fine wire. He threaded an end of this into some part of the device, fixed the spool in place on a spindle, and pressed a switch. There was a soft hum. The screen lighted.

In glowing, vivid colors a scene took form. At the same time there was a slow swelling of music. Two lines of men and women dressed in gay costumes faced each other against a vast painted backdrop. The costumes and setting depicted a symbolism, which I could not grasp, but the nature of the scene was evident enough, suggesting opera or ballet. As the music rose in volume, the men and women bowed to each other, and then moved together, merging, to separate as couples. A quick, sprightly dance began, with the couples gyrating in a pulse-lifting rhythm, forming intricate changing patterns. The music, bright and lilting in tempo, wove the color and movement of the spectacle into a harmonious, fascinating composition.

The settings and the music changed from time to time. Occasionally only one couple danced, and then singing would be featured, solo and chorus. My interest gradually waned as I found myself growing sleepy. I glanced at Burdeen, to note his own reactions. But he was watching Varis, as he had watched her more or less continually the entire time.

Finally the program ended, the screen darkening, the music fading into silence. Julon rose to drop the tapestry back in place. With a gravely apologetic smile, he indicated that he sensed the weariness of Burdeen and myself, and that we would be excused if we wished to sleep. We nodded our acceptance. After an exchange of smiles and bows, Elvar led us to the sleeping chamber where earlier we had washed.

Burdeen and I chose our respective beds, removed our coveralls, and lay down, pulling up around ourselves thick warm blankets. Elvar nodded at us and went out, extinguishing the lights. We were alone with our thoughts in the darkness.

After a while Burdeen said: "Gilroy."

"What is it?"

"Have you figured out what happened to us yet?"

"Not yet," I said. "But I have a vague idea. I'd rather not explain it, though, until I'm sure."

"Suppose we have to stay here—for good?"

"We'll just have to make the best of it, I guess."

"Living here wouldn't be so bad."

I said slowly, "Don't you want to go back?"

Burdeen was silent a moment. Then he said, "Yes, I want to go back. This is a nice place—but it isn't our world."

We said nothing more. I fell asleep, thinking, as it seemed I would always think, of Suzanne.

The days that followed were filled with various activities. Burdeen and I were introduced to the other leaders of the people in the valley, who formed a sort of governing council of which Julon was the head. We were taken on tours of the city and to numerous banquets. The others, like Julon, seemed anxious to know the purpose of our visit. It meant something to them that I couldn't grasp. I think it was this lack of understanding on our part, coupled with our inability to explain, that led Julon and his associates to take an extremely important step where Burdeen and I were concerned.

WE WERE taken one morning to a large marble building, which seemed to be a kind of university or school. In the room to which we were led were two chairs, each literally festooned with a bewilderingly complex array of apparatus. By means of gestures, Julon gave us to understand that were to occupy the chairs. He endeavored to make it clear that we were not to be harmed, and that whatever was to take place would be to our advantage.

The apparatus, however, was not reassuring. I surveyed it somewhat anxiously and glanced at Burdeen. He shrugged slightly.

"They're going to do something to us," I whispered. "I don't think it will hurt. Let's give them the benefit of the doubt anyway."

We sat down in the chairs, and two assistants began to fasten various portions of the apparatus about our heads. Metal skullcaps wound with wires were placed over our hair, a kind of earphones upon our ears, and over our eyes thick, cumbersome spectacles, through which I could at first see nothing. Finally the touch of hands left us. We waited tensely for what was to happen next.

There was an abrupt hum in my ears, a flash of light and color before my eyes. My head became oddly weightless. My thoughts, as I considered these sensations, seemed strangely keen and vigorous. It was as though my powers of concentration had been heightened. This, as I learned afterward, was what actually happened, by a process of subduing all superfluous thought and emotion save those concerning matters immediately at hand.

The light before my eyes steadied. The image of a man appeared. Even as I realized this, a word in strange letters appeared below the image, and a word, obviously the same as the written one, was spoken in my ear. The image of the man walked, ran, smiled, became angry, each action being both visually and audibly described. And with my increased powers of thought and concentration, I found that I retained a perfect memory of each explanation. I knew that I would be able easily to understand the words if I should ever hear them spoken or see them written.

Additional subjects followed. Animals, houses, trees, and other things of a simple nature. Thus began the education of Burdeen and myself in the language of the people of the valley. As the days passed, we learned quite rapidly. How much of our speedy progress can be credited to the mental aid given by the teaching apparatus, or to our already vague familiarity with the language, is uncertain. Chaucer wouldn't have had much difficulty in learning modern English—even less if he'd had a device to bolster and stimulate his thought processes while learning.

Before long Burdeen and I were able to hold simple conversations with the others. We didn't attempt to question them as yet, nor did they attempt to question us. By a sort of tacit agreement, we were waiting until the time when our vocabularies would be most nearly equal. This would permit a more complete and thorough discussion of the things important to us.

Burdeen and I managed, however, to learn many things through these early conversations. We were still on Earth, not on a planet in some remote corner of the Universe, as we had dimly feared. From the changes, which had taken place, it was obvious that a very long time had passed. This bore out the suspicion that I'd held about time being involved somehow in the flight. But how much time was impossible to determine.

The valley and the city were known comprehensively as Ard. The same name applied also to the planet as a whole, but among Julon and his people it applied particularly to the city. The government of Ard was essentially democratic, the councilors and their presiding head being chosen by vote of the people. But life in Ard was so simple and well ordered that the tasks of government were practically nonexistent. Machines did all the work, produced all the goods. Everyone had everything he needed, and no person had any more than the other.

FREED from labor by the machines, the people of Ard used leisure to excellent advantage. They had made many advances in science and technology. Their music, literature, drama, and art were imaginatively vigorous and distinctly original. They had innumerable mind, body, and character building activities in the way of sports, contests, and hobbies. Their time, in fact, was in every way occupied beneficially.

I had earlier supposed from what I had thought was their reliance upon machines that the Ardians were sinking gradually into decadence. I had learned that was the fate that usually befell people who were cared for without effort of their own. But far from sinking into decadence, the Ardians were arising from it.

The machines were not a development of their own. It seems that the machines, like the great empty cities and the planet itself, had always been. The cities and the planet had gradually been deserted. Those who had remained had come to rely too completely upon the machines, and when the machines had stopped, they had lapsed into barbarism. The Ardians, at some time in the distant past, had learned slowly and painfully to repair, start, and operate the machines again. They had not fallen into their old ways, but had used the machines as stepping stones to even greater achievements.

A lot of time had passed, of course, during the period from decline to resurgence. During that time, freed from the bonds of print, the English language had undergone more changes than had taken place throughout the several thousand years preceding. The Ardian tongue had seemed vaguely familiar to me, but no more. The educating apparatus, one of the ancient devices, which the Ardians had learned to use along with the others, had naturally been changed to conform to their own dialect. I wondered occasionally how large a role the educating apparatus had played in the Ardian rebirth.

I was a scientist, and these things were interesting to me. I discussed them—haltingly at first, to be sure—with many of the elders in Ard, and particularly with Julon. Talking with Julon made me understand why he had been chosen a leader. His mind was very keen, and he had studied intensively the record-spools of the ancients. He possessed not only an amazingly broad range of knowledge, but the sense of human values and perspectives, coupled with a truly objective attitude, necessary to apply it.

Such of my time as was not spent under the educating apparatus was passed in this way. I made few friends outside of Julon and the other elders. As for Burdeen, he was occupied in a manner typical of him. He entered zestfully into the sports and physical contests of Ard, natural outlets for his restless, competitive spirit. His great strength and stubborn endurance soon made him the idol of the city's youth. And I noted that he was often with Varis.

Finally the education of Burdeen and myself was completed. It was an event for which Julon had long and impatiently been waiting. After breakfast on the morning of the day following our "graduation", he asked us to accompany him to the garden at the rear of the house. We settled ourselves on a marble bench that circled a small pool.

It was cool, with that crisp tang to the air I'd grown to know so well. It was always cool, even when the reddish sun hung at zenith. There was a light wind. In the surrounding trees birds twittered and chirped quarrelsomely.

JULON glanced slowly at Burdeen, and then at me. He seemed more than ordinarily grave. After a moment he said:

"My friends, there are things which we of Ard have wanted to know ever since your arrival here. But first I shall tell you the reasons, so that you will understand us.

"You have undoubtedly seen the world as it is...a waste of snow and ice, for the most part. The world is almost deserted. There are some people left, but these are savages, living in crude houses of wood and skins, or skulking among the crumbling towers of the ancient cities. There are none such as the people of Ard. Our kind is alone in the world—and the world is growing cold and inhospitable. If our descendants are to advance and grow and become a mighty race, we must leave Ard and find a habitable planet circling a younger, warmer sun.

"In the dim past, men had machines—much like your own machine—in which to travel the vast distances between the stars. That is why the world is deserted now. They found and settled fresh, new planets, and as the old world grew cold, others left one by one to join them. Those who remained depended upon the servant-mechs, and when the servant-mechs broke down, they became savages." Julon looked up at the sky, and his tone became faintly bitter.

"All the available space machines were taken in the exodus. There were many more people, in fact, than there were space machines. That is why some remained behind. It was not of their choosing. A part of them, however, managed to gather the record-spools, which explained the construction of space machines. These built the machines they needed and left. But they either took with them or destroyed the all-important record-spools. Subsequently refugees were left stranded. We of Ard wish to leave this world for a new one among the stars, but the means with which to do so is beyond our grasp. We do not know, as did the ancients, how to build space machines.

"Out of our thwarted hopes a legend grew—a legend that some day men would come from the stars to visit the planet of their birth. They would find us of Ard, and would take us to the new world we sought. Or if they could not take us, they would give us the vital secrets of building space machines." Julon gazed at Burdeen and me in sudden, intense appeal. It shocked me a little, for he had always seemed so profound and self-sufficient.

"My friends, it is obvious that you have come from the stars. Now that you know our plight, will you not help us? All we ask is that you teach us to build a space machine like your own, so that we may find a new home—so that what we have started here in Ard will not perish when the sun finally dies."

I glanced in dismay at Burdeen. There was a serious flaw in the *Starling's* warp-line principle. If our short flight had had such an effect upon ourselves, what more serious results might it not have from a voyage across the immense gulf between the stars, as Julon contemplated? And while Burdeen and I knew the construction of space vessels, it was the construction of interplanetary vessels—not of interstellar vessels, which were what Julon had in mind.

Julon saw from our expressions that something was wrong. "What is it?" he asked. "Can you not help us?"

The question could not be avoided. I sighed, regretting the disappointment my words would bring, and launched into an account of the *Starling's* incredible flight.

Julon was silent for a long while after I finished. Then he said dully:

"You have not come from the stars. You have come from this world—the world of long ago."

"And the difficulty is," I answered helplessly, "that we don't even know how. A lot of time has passed. I know that time is involved—but I don't know how."

JULON rested an elbow on his knee and stared at the grass, considering the matter. It was as though the problem of his people were no longer uppermost in his mind. At last he said:

"I have done much studying of the ancient record-spools. I know many of the things that the ancients knew—and some, which they had forgotten or overlooked in the dense growth of new knowledge around them. I think I have the answer to that which puzzles you. It involves an ancient theory—the theory of relativity. The man to whom it is credited is no longer known."

I straightened on the bench, electrified, a name ringing in my mind. The name was Einstein. It was all suddenly very clear to me. I knew what Julon was going to say even as he said it.

"According to the theory of relativity," he went on, "time is a function of the velocity of light. Time, that is to say, is a relative quantity depending on the position of the observer— whether at rest or in motion. In motion, the time interval slows as speed is increased. As the speed of light is approached, time slows so greatly that it becomes negligible.

"But it is all relative. To the observer in motion, it is not apparent that time is passing at a faster rate than that to which he is accustomed. The instruments, which measure time, move at the usual rate. The bodily processes continue as normal. But—for each tiny interval measured off by the instruments, for each beat of the heart, of the observer in motion, hundreds of years pass with respect to the observer at rest.

"That is what happened to you, my friends. During the half hour while you traveled at a speed near that of light, many thousands of years passed here, upon the slower moving world."

I sat as though frozen, stunned into immobility. How could Alward and I possibly have overlooked that fact? It seemed too fantastic for belief—but we had. I can only explain it this way. The theory of relativity was old when Alward and I built the *Starling*. It had been buried amid a welter of others on the nature of time and space, which had arisen through the years. And the work on the *Starling* had been so complicated and exhausting that we had been able to think of nothing beyond the immediate principles involved. Or perhaps the full truth is simply that Alward and I had gazed so long upon the bright light of our dream that we had been blinded to everything else. It was not the first time that important, fundamental truths had been overlooked in the too zealous pursuit of a goal.

But exactly how the omission had taken place was not important. What mattered most to me, once I knew what had happened, was whether or not it was possible for Burden and me to return to the period from which we had come.

"Time," I muttered, turning abruptly to Julon. "Time! Julon, the ancients were very wise. Didn't they ever discover how to travel in time?" The thought was exhilarating in the hopes it offered. I would be able to see Suzanne again. And after Alward had found a way to correct the flaw in the principle of the *Starling*, Burdeen and I could return to help Julon and his people.

But Julon shook his head. "I have never found any record-spools which discussed travel in time. I doubt that the ancients ever discovered it at all. Time is merely an extension of space, a relative quantity arising from motion in space. It is not, like space, a tangible or available medium for travel."

Everything went out of me. I felt empty and cold, unutterably desolate.

It was checkmate. Julon could not help us, nor could we help him, we were stranded here.

CHAPTER FIVE
A Vital Discovery

NOTHING more was said for a long while. I stared blindly at the grass, thinking in despair of what Julon had said. Abruptly I grew conscious of what seemed at the moment a glaring inconsistency. I turned sharply to Julon. He looked at me with an evident glow of hope in his eyes.

According to what you say," I told him, "travel in time is impossible. Yet Burdeen and I reached this era by a method which is essentially time travel. We underwent a passage forward in time."

Julon shook his head with slow emphasis. "You confuse the meaning of the term. You are thinking of time as a cause rather than as an effect. The method by which you reached this era was not a true passage through time, but the result of the effect upon your time rate of speed approaching that of light."

"But," I persisted, "the fact still remains that Burdeen and I accomplished what in a sense may be called traveling in time."

Julon smiled slightly and shrugged. "In a sense, yes."

"Then if there is a passage forward in time, there ought to be a passage backward. It should operate both ways like everything else."

"The assumption is logical, but it does not hold good under the conditions which you call time travel. You moved forward in time, because your motion at close to light speed slowed your time rate with respect to that of observers on the world you left. Thus thousands of years passed for them, while only a half-hour passed for you. Now, keeping in mind this condition, suppose we reverse the process to effect what you hope would be a passage backward in time. You would have to attain a motion approaching absolute rest, as you had in the beginning attained a motion approaching absolute speed—the speed of light. Thus a half-hour would pass here...while thousands of years passed for you. Under the conditions postulated, there can be no other result, no other course."

"It's hopeless," Burdeen said. "You might as well forget the whole thing, Gilroy."

I shook my head. "It seems hopeless—but only under the conditions given." I turned back to Julon. "Suppose we base our assumptions upon a different set of conditions— conditions under which a passage backward in time would be as logical as had been the passage forward under the conditions we've discussed?"

"What would be the nature of these new conditions?" Julon asked.

"I don't know," I said. "I only know that they would necessarily lie outside this space-time continuum. We might reason as follows: Terming our space-time continuum normal space, then acceleration in normal space approaching that of light leads to negative acceleration in time. That is, the time rate of the observer in motion with respect to that of an observer at rest, at the departure point, is slowed.

"Now we might assume the existence of a different space-time continuum, which we shall call negative space, where effects are exactly opposite to those in this space. Then acceleration in negative space would still lead to negative acceleration in time—but it would be negative time. Thus if we were to follow as closely as possible the circumstances of the first flight, traveling for half an hour at close to light speed, the flight in negative space would take us back in time almost exactly the same amount which we had undergone in the passage forward."

"A clever idea," Julon said. "Unfortunately, it is impossible to accomplish in fact. We know of no way to reach these outer spaces of which you speak."

A SUDDEN thought occurred to me. It seemed merely a random notion, in no way linked to the subject at hand. But it persisted, and after a moment, in a flash of realization, I saw how it might be the exact thing I needed.

I grasped Julon's arm. "We know of no way to reach those other spaces—but the ancients did! Look, Julon, by your own words, the ancients possessed interstellar travel. It could not have taken place through this space, since the time effect in combination with the enormous distances between the stars, would have taken them in time to a point where the Universe no longer existed. And they could not have traveled at a safe minimum below the speed of light, because a voyage under that condition would have taken many lifetimes. They could only have accomplished it by passing through some other space-time, where the time effect did not obtain, or where interstellar distance were contracted."

"Yes," Julon said, a dawning eagerness in his eyes. "Yes!"

"We've got to search," I said, shaking his arm in my vehemence. "Somewhere there is a record-spool which explains about these other space-times. We've got to find it. You and your people have overlooked it before, blinded by your desire for space machines, never realizing that the secret was in your possession all the while."

"There is a chance that you may be right," Julon said. "We may have overlooked this knowledge. But if it exists at all, we shall find it." There was grim determination in his tone. He rose purposefully from the bench, and with renewed hopes Burdeen and I followed.

A special meeting was held in the council building that afternoon. Every Ardian had been called upon to attend.

Julon lost no time in explaining the purpose of the meeting. Speaking slowly, as though to impress upon the gathering the importance of his words, he recounted the discussion, which he had held with Burdeen and me that morning, and the decision to which it had led. Finally, he detailed the nature of the search, which had to be undertaken, emphasizing the fact that no clue however slight was to be ignored.

The meeting ended on a note of high enthusiasm. The Ardians seemed delighted with the opportunity that had arisen, slim as were its chances for success.

As the chamber cleared of its excited throng, Julon turned to Burdeen and me. He said, "We will now return to the house. With the project under way, I wish to investigate my own record-spool collection. I cannot recall any dealing with the subject of space-time, but it is possible that I have overlooked or forgotten them."

It proved to be no easy task, for Julon's library was quite extensive. The record-spools were but little larger than spools of thread, and it was amazing how many of them could be contained in a relatively small space. Like books once had been, they were titled according to the nature of their subject matter, but an examination of the titles alone was not enough, since what we sought might have been touched upon briefly, or contained in a paragraph or so of digressive material. We were thus compelled to run most of the record-spools through spectacle-like reading devices.

Several days passed in this manner. To avoid eyestrain, we took frequent periods of rest. And we read with painstaking slowness through the collection so as to miss nothing. But we found not even so much as a mere mention of the information we sought. Only the knowledge that some seeker among the other Ardians might turn up something kept me from sinking completely into despair.

THE others reported one by one to Julon. For the most part, they had been no more successful than ourselves. Some thought they had discovered the desired facts, but these turned out upon examination to have no relation to what we wanted. A few turned in with more worthwhile results, but the information in the record-spools they brought, contained in a few sentences or so, was too brief or tenuous to be valuable. I was fully convinced that the quest was doomed to failure, when one of the Ardians brought in a record-spool, which changed everything.

At first I could not see how it could possibly be important. The spool was a travelogue of a sort, relating the wonders of the various ancient cities. In the few passages that had any value, the author told of a wonderful machine contained within the Science Building in the city of Shago. His name for the machine was "The Omni-mech", which in our tongue means almost nearly "all-wise machine." It seems that a group of ancient scientists, realizing that the increasing dependence of the people upon the servant-mech would lead eventually to a dark age when these finally stopped, constructed a machine-brain which would embody all human knowledge. The Omni-mech was thus a pseudo-living encyclopedia. Its purpose was to inform and guide, from the simple questions and problems, which a savage would have, to the more intricate and detailed difficulties of a people as highly advanced as the Ardians. The idea was that the machine had a sort of involuntarily ability to raise back to the civilized level a people who had fallen into barbarism. Whether or not it had succeeded in this purpose was not revealed.

The full significance of the machine burst upon me in a flash. The ancient scientists who constructed it had obviously known the method of access to space-time continua other than this one, and since the machine embodied all the knowledge of that time, it was evident that this information would be contained along with everything else! Exultation roared through me like a great wind. The secret we sought had not been irretrievably lost after all. Return to the Earth I knew—to Suzanne—was something no longer relegated entirely to the realm of the impossible.

Nor was the importance of the machine, interpreted in his own way, lost upon Julon. His face lighted in incredulous joy. "Space machines!" he whispered. "At last the secret is within reach!"

I gripped Julon's shoulder eagerly. "We must go to Shago," I said. "We must find the Omni-mech."

He nodded slowly, sobering. "We will go—but there will be grave danger to us."

"Danger? What do you mean?" I demanded.

"Shago is inhabited by a tribe of savage degenerates," Julon said. "This much was learned by the few explorers who have been there—and who were fortunate enough to return alive. The degenerates worship the machines in Shago, considering the entire city holy ground. They are very ruthless toward intruders. If we are discovered, it is likely that we shall never live to return with anything we learn."

CHAPTER SIX
Disaster in Shago

ON A gray and dreary morning, we flew eastward in the *Starling* toward the ancient city of Shago. Space within the vessel, limited to begin with, was cramped, due to the fact that Julon and Elvar accompanied us. The discomfort was no great problem, however, since the speediness of the ship would bring us quickly to our destination.

Two days had passed following our decision to visit the city in quest of the Omni-mech and the precious information it contained. We had spent the time poring over old maps—maps of the country and of the city—and gathering together the equipment we would need. We had heavy clothing to wear in the bitter cold, a supply of food to tide us over should our search take longer than anticipated, flying belts, and long cylinders like over-sized ancient flashlights, which released atomic force. These latter were ingenious devices. By manipulating a tiny switch on the handle, the force could be controlled in intensity, so that the device served at once as a lighting and heating unit, a weapon, or as a cutting tool which pierced the hardest metals as easily as wax.

Because of his age, there had been some reluctance on the part of Burdeen and myself to include Julon. When our excitement had vanished sufficiently to enable us to view the expedition in a more practical light, we had realized that a young man would be of more value. But Julon had insisted firmly on going with us, pointing out that someone would be needed to guard the ship while we were gone, and that an old man would serve as well as a young one. To prove his point, he had given us a demonstration of his dexterity in handling the atomic cylinders, adjusted to weapon intensity, which had quickly convinced us that he would be fully the asset that he claimed. We had not been able to take along any further persons, since four in addition to the equipment was the *Starling's* full capacity.

It was with chaotic emotions that I watched, in the view-plate, the country flash by below us. Elation surged through me at the thought that Suzanne might soon no longer be just a memory, just an abstraction, but real and near. Then I thought of Shago and the wonderful machine in the Science Building called the Omni-mech, and fear grew heavy and cold inside me. Suppose the machine had deteriorated through the years—suppose the degenerate inhabitants of the city had damaged it?

With an effort, I forced myself into some measure of calm. Worrying solved nothing, I realized. Time only would show the destruction or fulfillment of our hopes.

I glanced at Burdeen, sitting next to me, fingers resting with a sort of detached attention upon the controls. His brows were drawn in a faintly puzzled frown, as though thinking of something he didn't fully understand. It was easy enough to guess what was on his mind, for his expression was one he frequently wore when gazing at Varis. She seemed to bewilder him, awakening emotions within him that conflicted with his natural impulses. When with her, he was strangely quiet and kind, not at all like the dashing, possessive Burdeen I remembered.

The reasons for his behavior seemed understandable. He loved Varis, as one could not help but love her, but he must have realized it could lead to nothing in the end. Like myself, his thoughts and desires were all for returning to the Earth of the time we knew as home. He wished to do nothing, which when the time for departure came—if it ever did—would cause the girl regrets. And it puzzled him.

Nor were Burdeen and I the only reflective ones. Julon and Elvar were watching the view-plate, but from the fixed blankness of their eyes, I knew they didn't really see it. They were looking into vast distances beyond, thinking, surely, of the stars and of the new home they hoped to find there.

THE warp generators hummed softly in the bemused silence that filled the control room. The ship was some twenty thousand feet high, traveling at a speed close to six hundred miles an hour. We could, of course, have gone more rapidly, but this would have made difficult the finding of the landmarks, which were to guide us to the city. It must be remembered that the land had changed. Most of the old rivers and lakes were gone. Some followed new courses, while others had become frozen in the intense cold of the north and covered over with snow.

We had been following the coast eastward along the Gulf of Mexico. Finally we reached one of our landmarks, the mouth of a great river running at right angles to our course. The river was not the Mississippi. It lay some three hundred miles east of where the Mississippi had been. The city was located in an almost straight line from the mouth of the river, and would now be easy to find.

Burdeen swung the ship north. We dropped closer to the ground, our speed slackening. The vast forests below us, spreading away on either side of the river began to thin. Snow began to cover the ground more and more thickly. Immense glaciers gleamed dully in the wan light of the sun.

At last we reached Shago, looking from above like a huge gray-blue stain against the white fabric of the snow. It was not the city Burdeen and I had seen upon our return. It was many times larger and taller, if possible, than that first city had been. Full awareness of its stupendous size came to us dazedly as we descended. The eye could not grasp all of it at once. There was just a general impression of gigantic metal towers, shining in soft pastel hues, and a network of inter-connecting aerial spans that dropped down level after level toward the ground.

The vastness and complexity of the city beat at us like a tangible force. Then, as we floated down toward the towers, we grew conscious of something else. It was the quietness of the city, the utter lack of motion. The stillness seemed to hold a subtle air of menace, as though inimical presences lurked in hiding among the shadows.

Julon pointed abruptly at the view-plate. "There it is!" he said. "The Science Building."

We could hardly have missed it. The Science Building was located almost in the center of the city, its spire reaching hundreds of feet higher than the others all around it. As we drew closer, we made out more distinctly the metal statue surmounting it. The statue depicted the figure of a man in the act of leaping, one arm outstretched, a symbolization of Man's eager quest for knowledge. From the descriptions given by the record-spool dealing with the Omni-mech, the building had been easy to find.

Burdeen landed the ship upon a topmost terrace of the building, which the fierce winds at that height had kept relatively free of snow. We donned heavy hooded jackets and strapped the flying devices to our shoulders. Then each grasping an atomic cylinder, we were ready to leave. Julon, who was to remain on guard at the ship, saw us off with a word of caution.

"You will have to hurry. If the degenerate inhabitants of the city have seen us arrive, they will come to investigate."

With Julon's warning an ominous echo in my ears, I followed Burdeen and Elvar from the ship. Instantly, as I stepped outside, a fierce cold wind smashed at me, hurling me almost to my knees. I braced myself with frantic haste against the ship's hull, a vision flashing through my mind of being blown from the terrace to a horrible death on the ground over a thousand feet below. I gasped for breath, the wind roaring past my face in a constant gale. A terrible cold began to close around me, like the grip of a giant fist of ice.

Burdeen shouted something. He had to repeat it before I understood him over the howl of the wind.

"Down! How are we going to get down?"

"Through the building," I yelled. "It's the only way."

IT HAD been our intention to descend on our flying apparatus along the side of the building, seeking an entrance on one of the lower floors. But the wind rendered this impossible. We would have been blown away helplessly in the attempt.

A short distance from where we stood was a series of long narrow windows. They were not windows as we understood them, for they were flush and continuous with the wall, merely transparent portions of it. Inching over to one of the windows, we adjusted our atomic cylinders to the proper intensity and began to cut a circular opening large enough, for us to squeeze through.

Nor was the task before us any simpler once we reached the interior, since the building was a veritable maze of chambers and halls. We knew that the Omni-mech was located on a lower floor, near the ground level, but we could at first find no arrangement, which would permit a descent. We wandered through numerous and seemingly endless halls before we came at last to one where, in the center, the opening of a circular shaft gaped.

The bottom of the shaft, as we peered down, was lost in shadows. Spaced at intervals around its walls were vertical rails. Understanding of the purpose of the shaft came to me after a moment. It was similar to an elevator shaft of familiar memory, save that ascent and descent were accomplished by individual apparatus, like the flying devices, instead of by a car. When one reached the floor of his destination, he simply grasped a rail and swung himself out of the shaft.

I gestured at the opening. "We can go down through here, on our flying belts," I told Burdeen and Elvar. "But first we'd better leave direction markers to help us find the ship when we return."

Our wanderings had given us a rough idea of the plan of the chambers and halls. Without much difficulty, we found the window through which we had entered the building, and blazed a trail back to the shaft by searing guide marks at intervals along the walls and floors with our atomic cylinders. Then, switching on our flying devices, we began the descent.

Slowly we floated down through increasing darkness, amid a silence so deep it was uncanny, the flying devices bearing us as easily as feathers. They functioned on a principle somewhat similar to that of the *Starling,* save that they warped gravity instead of space. And they were, of course, marvelously light and compact. By comparison Alward's warp generators were crude and ponderous constructions.

In our descent we discovered plaques fastened to the rails, numbering off the various floors. These guided us to the floor where, according to the record-spool, the Omni-mech was located. Our search even then was hardly simplified, since the building increased in width toward the base and this part of it contained several times as many chambers and halls as toward the top. Finally, however, we came to a chamber, which by its size alone indicated its importance. And it was lighted. Huge globes in the ceiling shed a bright steady radiance over even the farthest walls.

We had been using our atomic cylinders for illumination. Now we switched them off, peering in wondering silence about us.

What we had seen of the Science Building so far had shown us that it was a sort of museum, containing specimens and exhibits of every scientific achievement known to the ancients. If such it actually was, then the machine, which occupied most of the chamber, must surely have been its chief attraction. At first glance it resembled nothing so much as a squat pyramid, narrowing in tiers toward the top. Then the eye took in separate details, the bewildering complexity of wheels, gears, wires, and tubes which made up the entire mass—all glinting and shining in the light.

A sudden current of eagerness raced through me. The machine was the Omni-mech. Even if I hadn't had the description of the record-spool to go on, I should have known from the size and intricacy of the machine that it couldn't be anything else.

GESTURING excitedly to Burdeen and Elvar, I strode forward. The machine seemed to rise up before me as the basis of comparison shifted gradually from the vast chamber to myself. When I had approached close enough, I saw that a certain fear, which I had entertained, was groundless, for the Omni-mech had not been damaged. Thought of this brought abrupt recollection of the degenerates. We had lost a lot of time in locating the machine. Now we would have to hurry, since there was always the possibility that the degenerates had seen the *Starling* arrive. If they actually worshipped machines as Julon had said, then merely touching the Omni-mech would be considered the highest sacrilege.

Burdeen strode up to my side. "What are you going to do?" he asked. "How are you going to get the information we want."

"There's supposed to be a place where one can get into communication with the Omni-mech," I said. "We'll find it, and then—"

"There!" Elvar said, pointing. "See the stairs?"

Following the direction of his arm, I saw a flight of narrow, ladder-like steps leading up to the first tier of the machine. I nodded. "That seems to be the place. I'll go up and see what I can accomplish. Burdeen, you and Elvar had better remain down here and keep a close watch for the degenerates. They may not have seen the ship, but we can't take any chances."

While the two posted themselves on guard, I quickly mounted the steps, reaching a narrow space at the top, which was enclosed on three sides by wall-like partitions. A section of the flooring beneath my feet gave a little, startling me.

And then, as though to increase further my dismay, a sudden vast hum arose from somewhere deep within the machine, and simultaneously, tubes at various places glowed into life. I smiled wryly as I realized that my weight upon the floor had awakened the Omni-mech into activity.

I studied the panel before me. Set in it at various places was enigmatic slots and openings. Before I could so much as guess the purposes of these, a voice spoke—a soft, metallic voice that seemed to issue from somewhere close beside me.

"You have come for knowledge," the voice said. "Tell me how I may serve you."

I stared rather wildly about me, half expecting to see some strange being at my side. But I was still very much alone. In another moment I awoke to the fact that the voice had sounded from one of the openings in the panel before me. And it had spoken in English—oddly accented, perhaps, but still very much like the English to which Burdeen and I were accustomed.

I decided quickly on a course of action. The information desired by Julon was comparatively more simple than my own, and would show me what to expect by testing the ability of the Omni-mech.

Accordingly, I voiced in English a wish to obtain complete plans, details, and specifications of the interstellar vessels possessed by the ancients.

When I had finished, the machine spoke again. "The knowledge you wish will be given."

The humming of the machine seemed momentarily to deepen. Wheels turned and tubes brightened with an air of subdued, efficient activity. Suddenly there was a clicking sound from the panel before me. A soft rustle followed, and an object moved into sight through one of the slots.

"It is done," the Omni-mech said.

The object was a bound, thick sheaf of papers. There were diagrams and illustrations, and pages of mathematical and explanatory material. Even a short scrutiny showed that the information was so simply and clearly given that translating it into material form would hardly be a difficult task.

The hopes of Julon and his people now seemed definitely on the road to fulfillment. But my own? Would the Omni-mech be able to help me?

"There is something else that I wish to know," I told the machine.

"Tell me how I may serve you," it requested again.

I OUTLINED the story of how Burdeen and I had arrived in this era, then explained the theory of negative space by which I hoped to effect a return to our own time. "What I want to know," I concluded, "is whether a condition such as negative space exists, and if so, how can access to it be accomplished?"

The Omni-mech hummed thoughtfully for a while. Finally it said:

"Mathematics shows the concept of negative space to be tenable. I base my conclusion upon an extension of the Hyperspace Equations, which have made possible interstellar travel. The Equations serve as the framework for all other orders of space-time, but the fact that such an extension is possible indicates an important link. It may very well be that hyperspace is a sort of dividing line between this and negative space.

"The method of access to hyperspace shows that access to other orders of space-time is also possible. As the Hyperspace Equations serve as a framework, so does this method of access serve as a key. But my knowledge of other orders of space-time does not exceed these fundamentals. I have the foundation—but not the necessary structure above. Thus I lack the vital factors with which to formulate a method of access to negative space. I cannot help you."

Despair almost like sickness rushed over me. The Omni-mech was unable to help after all. There could be no return—exile was permanent. And Suzanne was doomed forever to remain just a memory.

I turned in leaden bitterness to leave the platform. But in the next instant I halted as an idea flashed into my mind. I whirled back to the panel.

"Perhaps I can supply the factors you need," I told the machine.

"New knowledge is always welcome. Proceed."

Slowly, carefully, so as to skip nothing, I detailed in mathematical terms the principle of Alward's warp generators. The Omni-mech digested this information with a humming note of deep interest. Abruptly the humming rose in pitch. Wheels turned and tubes brightened. If a machine could possibly display excitement, this was the time.

"You are correct. The factors you have given provide a solution. And they indicate an important relationship to the Hyperspace Equations, which leads me to believe that these are not fundamental after all, but a highly specialized development. They also bear out the existence of a link between hyperspace and negative space. Everything, in fact, seems connected with the warp principle which you have given."

"But the solution," I prompted impatiently, "I've got to know."

"The warp generators themselves provide the method of access. Only a few simple changes are needed. These will be explained in permanent form for later reference."

The machine hummed and clicked busily. Then through the slot where the previous one had appeared, a second bound sheaf of papers rustled into view. Though thinner than the first had been, it was to me infinitely more valuable.

I muttered a few hasty words of gratitude, and turned to hurry down the ladder. Burdeen and Elvar had forgotten their guard duties in their interest at what had been taking place. Their faces were stretched in broad grins of joy and relief.

I waved the papers at them.

"Here it is! Everything we want to know!"

AS THEY examined the papers curiously, I grew aware once more of the deep, unnatural silence of the building. The Omni-mech had quieted when I stepped from the platform. There was no sound now, save for the faint rustling of the sheets in the hands of Burdeen and Elvar.

And then, like a crash of lightning in the stillness, came a sudden clattering noise.

As one, we whirled. I heard Burdeen gasp. Elvar dropped the sheaf of papers he had been holding. I was conscious of these things with a strange clarity, even as my own body jerked in alarm.

Not thirty feet away stood a group of over a dozen men. They had evidently approached from the opposite side of the Omni-mech, moving so silently that we had not heard them. They were short, dark, squat, dressed barbarically in skins and furs. In their hands they held various crudely fashioned weapons, knives, spears, and fixed bows. They held these watchfully, as though prepared at any instant to use them. They stood there and looked at us out of hard little black eyes, set in faces that were brutish and cruel. They were, I knew instinctively, the degenerates of whom Julon had warned.

Burdeen whispered, "Get your atomic cylinders ready. It looks like we're going to have a fight on our hands to get out of here."

But as we reached slowly and cautiously for the devices, there was a guttural shout of command, and the degenerates leaped forward. They were incredibly fast and strong. Before we could do even so much as aim the atomic cylinders, they had reached us.

The struggle that followed was as short as it was futile. I was the first to go down, stunned by a blow to the temple. Burdeen and Elvar managed to hold out a while longer, but the odds were hopelessly against them. They were borne to the floor, stilled by blows and the sheer weight of numbers of our attackers.

Through a fog of semi-consciousness, I grew aware of being bound with rawhide thongs. Then I was carried outside. My senses cleared as the cold air hit me. On the snow before the building were a number of large sleds, drawn by huge shaggy dogs. Burdeen, Elvar, and I were tossed unceremoniously into one of the sleds. Orders were shouted, whips cracked. Whining, the dogs lunged in their traces. We were under way— bound for a destination that only our fierce captors knew.

I squirmed to a more comfortable position and glanced at Burdeen. His rugged features were pinched and bleak. He shook his head a little at me, said nothing.

Elvar was staring straight before him with a strange, fixed intensity, as though hypnotized. His expression frightened me. I called his name anxiously, but he didn't so much as flick his eyelids. Had a blow on the head injured his mind?

CHAPTER SEVEN
One Must Stay

THE runners of the sled moved smoothly and effortlessly over the snow. I could hear the degenerates talking or calling to each other in their thick guttural voices. They seemed vastly pleased. And occasionally the dogs of the different teams would bark eagerly in their attempts to out race each other.

I had a nightmarish sense of unreality. The city was like a fantastic jungle around us. The buildings seemed the boles of immense trees rising endlessly into the sky, the network of criss-crossing aerial spans overhead a tangle of huge lianas and vines. The twilight through which we moved heightened the illusion. Only a little of the weak sunlight ever managed to reach this level of the city.

The sleds drew up at last in a sort of courtyard formed by a group of buildings arranged in a circle. It didn't seem that we had traveled very far, certainly not over a mile or two.

The circular group of buildings seemed the quarters of the degenerates, for as the sleds entered the courtyard, people erupted from the doorways, gathering in a growing crowd around us. They fought to reach the sled in which Burdeen, Elvar, and I lay, shrilling excitedly. Those nearest pushed and plucked at us curiously. They were the same in dress and appearance as the band that had captured us. And I noticed that they smelled quite offensively.

With shouts and gestures, our guards finally cleared a circle around the sled. We were pulled roughly erect on the hard-packed snow. The bonds at our ankles were untied. Then, while part of the guards formed a moving wedge, the others dug their spears into our backs and marched us into one of the buildings.

The building seemed to be one of importance, for sentries were posted at numerous places within it. We were taken up a flight of stairs, down a short hall, and into a huge room. The floors were covered profusely with thick furs. Shields, spears, and swords hung upon the walls. Fires burned in two huge metal bowls set on each side of a massive carved chair. The smell of the burning wood did little to mask the strong, rank odor of the room.

In the chair, warmed by the fires in the flanking bowls, sat an old man. He was immensely fat. His fur garments were decorated lavishly with metal and bone ornaments. He stared at us with a kind of piggish interest out of little black eyes set deep in folds of pale flabby tissue. From the deferential way our guards bowed to him, I decided he was a chief or king.

In raspy, arrogant tones, the old man voiced a question. The leader of the guards launched into an explanation, gesticulating animatedly. When he had finished, he advanced to the chair, holding out the atomic cylinders and the two precious sheaves of instructions, which had been taken from us. The chief examined these. They didn't seem to mean anything to him. With a grunt of disdain, he handed them back to the guard and issued some decree concerning us that brought grins of animal delight to the faces of the others.

Burdeen, Elvar, and I were taken to a small adjoining room. Two degenerates stood guard at the door. They watched us with a sort of anticipatory gloating. Something was going to be done with us that gave these people a savage pleasure. It couldn't have been anything good.

Burdeen muttered, "Wonder what they're up to?"

"I'm trying not to think of it," I said.

"Do you suppose they're going to...kill us?"

"It looks that way. And indications are that they intend to get a lot of amusement out of it."

"Torture...?" Burdeen whispered.

181

I nodded slowly.

ELVAR didn't seem to be aware that we had spoken. Before we had been brought into the room, he had seemed almost his normal self, conscious of what was happening around him. But now he was once more staring fixedly into space, like one held in a trance. I called his name a few times, without results.

Burdeen asked, "What's the matter with him?"

"I don't know," I said. "I've never seen anything quite like it. He seems to have been frozen by shock."

Burdeen was silent for a while. Then he said:

"Julon is our only hope. He might grow worried by our absence and search for us."

"He wouldn't know where to look," I said. "The city is too big. And he was too high up in the building to have noticed us being carried away."

Burdeen's face twisted in desperation. "Then we've got to do something! We can't just let them do...whatever they intend to do to us!"

"What can we do?" I asked.

With an inarticulate sound, Burdeen abruptly lunged against his bonds. Almost instantly the two guards left the door, leaping at him and pointing their spears at his body. He quieted. His face took on a hopeless resignation that wasn't good to see.

Faintly, from outside, came an excited babble of voices. I twisted around to glance through the one large window with which the room was provided. Through it I saw the fronts of other buildings some distance away. I realized that the building in which we were located faced upon the courtyard. The excited clamor was coming from there.

I don't know how much time passed. I sunk into an apathetic listlessness, only dimly aware of the boisterous tumult taking place outside.

Then the door opened and a number of degenerates strode purposefully in. Their faces had been painted in weird designs, as though for a ceremony of some kind. Burdeen, Elvar, and I were hauled to our feet and pushed at spear's end from the room. We were taken outside, to the courtyard. A sick emptiness filled me at what I saw there.

Approximately in the center three wooden posts had been driven into the hard-packed snow. Piled at the bases of each were mounds of brushwood.

We were going to be burned to death—and evidently while alive.

Despite our frenzied struggles, we were borne relentlessly to the posts and lashed immovably in place. The instruction sheets, which we had obtained from the Omni-mech and the atomic cylinders, were placed at our feet, useless things to be destroyed along with us. Nor had our flying devices been removed. Apparently they were considered parts of our clothing.

The degenerates gathered in a circle around us, a wall of leering, wolfish faces. There was a sudden booming of drums. The painted warriors who had bound us to the posts now began stamping and chanting in what was obviously a sort of victory dance. By degrees, the beat of the drums increased in tempo. The warriors danced faster, their feet thudding against the snow in a quickening staccato rhythm. The crowd took up the tuneless chant, and the surrounding buildings hurled it back.

It didn't seem real. It was like something out of a dream. In the heart of the greatest city the world had ever known, savage throwbacks to a dim primitive age danced and chanted.

And then the crowd parted to let a figure enter the ring. It was the fat old chief. In one pudgy hand he clutched a flaming torch.

In a pompous waddle, the chief strode to Elvar's stake, bent to ignite the brushwood. Elvar didn't seem at all concerned. He was looking upward, toward the sky.

THE chief paused a moment, glancing upward, too, as though to see what could possibly interest Elvar more than his own impending horrible death. He screamed, a thin bleating sound. Dropping the torch, he flung himself madly at the crowd, now a solid unmoving mass of flesh as it, too, stared up at the sky.

The drums had stopped. The chanting had stopped. A thick stifled silence layover the courtyard.

Overhead, dropping swiftly down, came the *Starling!*

With shouts and yells of fear, the crowd awoke into motion. Sheer press of numbers thwarted its concerted efforts to flee. It became a maddened beast, ripping and clawing at itself in wild unreasoning fright.

The *Starling* descended to within a few feet of the ground and swung in a great circle, its tapering nose plowing into the heaving mass of figures and spreading further pandemonium. It kept moving until the courtyard had been cleared of all who had been able to escape. The motionless figures of those who had been trampled were scattered numerously over the snow. Among them was the fat old chief who had ordered our deaths.

At last, a few feet from where we stood, the *Starling* came to rest. The entrance port opened, and Julon swung to the ground. He peered warily about him for a moment, the atomic cylinder gripped in his hands. But the degenerates hadn't yet recovered sufficient presence of mind to return. With a fleeting smile in our direction, Julon bent to pluck a knife from the belt of a nearby sprawled form. Then he ran over to us, sliced quickly at our bonds.

"Hurry!" Julon urged. "Into the vessel!"

I paused only long enough to snatch up the precious instruction sheets. Burdeen and Elvar gathered the atomic cylinders, and then we clambered into the ship.

Within seconds, Burdeen at the controls, we were rising into the air. With the familiar confines of the control room once more around me, everything that had happened seemed a fevered delusion. Only did the miracle of our escape strike home. I whirled on Julon.

"But how did you know what had happened?" I demanded. "How did you know where to find us?"

Julon smiled. "Elvar told me."

"You must surely be joking," I protested. "How could Elvar possibly have told you?"

"By telepathy, of course."

"Telepathy!" I gasped.

"Can it be that you know nothing of this science?" Elvar asked, surprised.

"I know it," I said. "But the people of my time never considered it a science." I understood suddenly Elvar's strange trance-like condition while we were held captive by the degenerates. It had not been the result of a blow on the head, as I had feared. He had merely been in telepathic contact with Julon.

"The studies of the ancients brought mental telepathy to the state of a science," Julon said. "But learning to use it efficiently is very difficult, and for most persons impossible. Elvar and I had the advantage of kinship, being father and son, and in addition we have been practicing ever since Elvar was a child."

"And the ship?" I said, aware of another inconsistency. "How did you know how to operate the ship?"

Julon shrugged. "I watched Dan Burdeen operate the controls, and merely imitated his motions. My mind has been trained to observe and remember," he smiled again. "That is another science of which we know. And now I should like to ask a question of my own. You have secured the information we need?"

"All of it," I said. I showed him the instruction sheets. They were not written in his language, but the diagrams and illustrations would be easy to follow. And I could always make such translations as were necessary, as they were not greatly technical. The interstellar vessels of the ancients had, in fact, been astonishingly simple machines, despite the magnitude and intricacy of the principles on which they operated.

AFTER a moment Julon looked up from the sheets. His eyes shone with a strange moistness. "Were it not for your coming, all this would never have been possible," he said. "How can my people and I ever thank you?"

"You must not try to thank me," I told him. "If thanks is due at all, it is to the Fate that wove the threads of our lives into this pattern."

Julon nodded slowly. "We might call it Fate. The more men learn of science and the Universe, the deeper grows the realization that the ordering of laws and forces is too perfect for mere blind chance. Who can deny that the hand which controls the destinies of atoms and suns does not occasionally reach to embrace human lives as well?" And his eyes, shining in gratitude that this might be, looked toward the stars.

The ship hummed on its way to Ard.

Our return, unharmed, and with the information, for which we had set out, was the cause for a delightful celebration. A huge banquet was given in our honor at the

Council Building that evening. Festivities lasted until far into the night. Exhausted physically and emotionally by the tumultuous events of the day, we were glad when an opportunity finally presented itself that would permit us to leave. I fell asleep almost as soon as I reached by bed.

The weeks that followed were busy ones. I didn't immediately begin any work on preparing the *Starling* for the return to our own time of Burdeen and myself. The adjustments were simple and could be performed at any time within a few hours. They involved merely a reversal in the winding of the warp generator armatures, a different alignment of the field coils, and certain changes in the power connections. These alterations wouldn't change greatly the operating principle of the ship; it would still travel by riding a warp in the fabric of space—but it would be negative space. As the force created by the generators reached a certain intensity, the warp would invert into negative space; and since the ship would be carried along by the warp, it too would be swung into negative space. To exit, it was only necessary to decrease the propelling force below the intensity, which had given entrance. It was as beautifully simple as all really great ideas are.

The time was spent mainly in company with Julon and a group of other learned Ardians, translating and clarifying the information given by the Omni-mech for the construction of an interstellar vessel. Everything, as we progressed, was recorded permanently on record-spools. When we had finished, the information compiled was arranged and classified according to a working plan and divided up among technicians, both human and mechanical.

With all this under way, my help was no longer needed. The Ardians were mechanical marvels, as evidenced by the fact that they had not only learned to repair and use the ancient machines, but had built others and in many cases improved on them. There was no doubt in my mind but that they would be able to conclude successfully the task, which had been started.

I got to work on the changes in the warp generators of the *Starling*. As I went more thoroughly over the instructions given me by the Omni-mech, the feeling that something was wrong took hold of me. It was only a vague suspicion, nothing that I could definitely explain. But a certainty that it was of vital importance made it persist.

It wasn't until the changes had been completed and Burdeen and I were beginning our preparations to leave that realization of what was wrong finally came.

Burdeen and I happened to be inside the *Starling*, packing away some of the things we intended to take back with us as souvenirs. I dropped a box I'd been holding, and it fell with a startling crash to the floor.

Burdeen whirled and took in the expression on my face. "Why...what's the matter?" he asked puzzledly.

I DIDN'T answer. Instead, I went to the place in the control room where I had left the instruction sheets. I went carefully over one of the mathematical expressions they contained, then seized a writing pad and stylus and performed certain calculations. A chill wind seemed to blow through me as I finished. The check-up had proven my realization correct.

Burdeen had followed me to the control room. "Say, what's wrong with you?" he demanded.

"Wrong?" I echoed dully. "Plenty's wrong. You see, one of us will have to stay here. For one of us there is to be no return."

Burdeen said slowly, "But why? What do you mean?"

"It's because of the changes we made in the warp generators," I said. "The operating principle remains basically the same, but in the translation to negative space, an entirely new factor has to be considered—the mass of the ship. As the propelling force created by the generators reaches a certain critical intensity, the inversion of the warp and consequent translation of the ship take place. But this critical intensity is a function of the mass of the ship. If its mass is over a maximum limit, inversion and translation fail to take place. Instead, a terrific strain upon the fabric of space would be created which would cause a collapse. As a result, we would be hurled into some alien space-time continuum from which we could never hope to return."

"And the ship is over this maximum mass limit?" Burdeen said.

I nodded. "By over two-hundred pounds."

"Couldn't we get rid of this excess weight by stripping the ship?"

"You know the answer to that as well as I do," I said. "Everything that wasn't absolutely necessary has already been removed. We might be able to discard a few parts here and there, but they certainly wouldn't total over two hundred pounds in weight. No—the solution I gave is the only one that can be considered. One of us has to stay."

"I weigh over two-hundred pounds," Burdeen said thoughtfully. His blue eyes turned grim and hard. "Listen, Gilroy, are you trying to trick me into staying here? If you're lying to me, I'll knock you from one end of the valley to the other."

"Take the instruction sheets and my calculations to Julon," I said. "Have him check them. He'll tell you the same thing I did."

The doubt left Burdeen's face. He looked at me, and I looked at him, and the same thought ran through our minds.

Which of us would be the one to remain?

CHAPTER EIGHT
The Long Way Home

IT WAS a fateful moment. Until now I had been too startled by my discovery to think of its possible effects upon my hopes of returning to Suzanne. Fear chilled me as I realized what might happen.

Burdeen wanted to return as badly as I did. That was evident from his restraint toward Varis. If he had been reconciled to the idea of remaining permanently in Ard, he certainly would have paid her more attention. But he had merely been kind to her, as a man will be kind to a girl when he has another on his mind. Like myself, he hadn't been able to forget Suzanne and the world from which we had come.

Now a return was possible—but only for one. For either of us to volunteer willingly to remain seemed out of the question. And I knew that Burdeen would no more gamble his chance than I would. It was too precious to risk. That eliminated such obvious solutions as choosing straws, contests of strength or intelligence, or leaving the decision to an impartial outsider.

The only way out of the dilemma seemed for one ruthlessly to exterminate the other. It was a conclusion at which a man of Burdeen's temperament would logically arrive. I recalled only too well the fear I'd felt on the morning just before the flight that Burdeen, aware Suzanne loved me, might try to get me out of the way by some means which would look like an accident. Nothing so complicated was necessary now. Burdeen could merely overpower me, reduce the weight of the ship by the additional amount needed, and leave. Back in our own time, he could simply explain that I had volunteered to remain behind. The explanation that I had fallen in love with Varis would satisfy Suzanne as to my reason for having done so.

I knew Burdeen was thinking thoughts similar to mine. And I knew he must already have decided on a course of action.

Only one of us would leave the control room. It would not be willingly. It would not even be while conscious—or alive.

And it would happen now, within seconds. Neither of us could allow the other any time to prepare an offensive.

Burdeen had been looking at me. A flicker crossed his face—warning of an impending motion. With the instantaneous reaction of tight-wound nerves, I leaped to the nearest pilot chair and poised my fingers over the control studs in its arm.

"Stop!" I snapped. "Come near me by so much as one single step, and I'll send the ship into an acceleration which will kill us both."

For a moment Burdeen looked puzzled. Then he smiled and shook his head. "Don't be a fool, Gilroy. If you have any ideas that I might force you to stay here, you can forget them."

"You're lying!" I said. "I know very well that you want to get back as badly as I do."

Burdeen shook his head again. His smile became faintly sad, faintly contemptuous. "You're wrong. You see, Gilroy, for a long time I've been torn between two desires—to stay here, and to return home. I just couldn't seem to make up my mind, but now it's been made up for me. I'm staying.

"This is the way I look at it. There'd be nothing for me if I went back. Suzanne loves you. I could win her over in time, but it would be only to share her with a memory—and I want all or nothing. And back home I was just a pilot—a good one, maybe, but good pilots are easy to find. Here, I'm a power behind the throne, so to speak. Julon and the others need me. They'll get their starship, but they don't know piloting or navigation. Somebody'll have to teach them that. Besides, I'd like to see the stars, and this is my chance," he paused a moment, as if in hesitation.

"And there's Varis. She's a sweet kid. I couldn't seem to make up my mind about her either, but now I know I love her. And I know she loves me. So there's no reason for me to want to go back. I know when I'm well off—even if it did take me quite a while to realize it."

Burdeen was sincere. His eyes and the tone of his voice told me that beyond any slightest doubt.

A wave of sudden shame beat over me. I had thought and acted like a melodramatic fool.

I don't know how I managed to overcome my pride, but I went over to Burdeen and held out my hand. I said awkwardly, "I'm sorry...Dan. I didn't know all this. I judged you according to my own feelings about the situation, and I know from experience that this is never a good guide to the other fellow's thoughts. I won't be so quick at jumping to conclusions next time."

Burdeen gripped my hand hard. "Forget it. I said and did some things that would give anybody the wrong ideas. Here's hoping you get home safely...Chuck."

I LEFT a few days later. To avoid excess weight, I had to discard many of the souvenirs I'd intended to take along. I had also to refuse gifts of food and flowers from the Ardians, which in quantity would have filled to bursting at least half a dozen ships the size of the *Starling*, I did, however, take with me several small light articles which would prove that Ard had actually existed. And there was a letter from Burdeen to Professor Alward, which in a moment of high spirits he had written in the form of a resignation.

Leaving was harder than I had anticipated. Julon, Mera, Elvar, and Varis had become my friends in the deepest sense of the word. And Ard, with its classical buildings and tall golden people, had after all been a very pleasant place. It was with a burning constriction in my throat that I shook hands all around and closed the entrance port against the farewell cries of those who had come to see me off.

I buckled my safety straps and watched the view-plate, waiting until the crowd had moved a safe distance away. The last thing I saw, as I took off, was Burdeen, waving, his arm around Varis. Though tiny in the view-plate, her face looked radiantly happy.

The tasks involving my return were not difficult. I had only to follow the original course the *Starling* had taken, being careful to accelerate and decelerate within the former time intervals. The translation into and out of negative space would occur automatically, as the intensity of the propelling warp rose toward and fell below the critical level. While in negative space, I would travel for a half-hour at close to light speed, so that the same amount of time would pass relative to Earth as had passed previously. Since this would be negative time, I would find, upon my landing, that I had returned to a period close to that from which I had left. In actual practice, however, I intended to travel at close to light speed for a little longer than a half hour, to make up for the time I had spent in Ard.

During the trip back, I was filled with constant anxiety that something might go wrong. That nothing actually did, I can only thank the Omni-mech—or Fate. Time—relative to myself, of course—seemed to drag like centuries. I found that I was able to stand the acceleration with less discomfort than on the first flight. It was as though my sojourn in Ard had toughened me.

Negative space proved to be disappointing. It looked almost exactly like normal space, except that there seemed to be fewer stars. The only sensations I experienced in the translation into and out of it were brief tingles throughout my body, as though every atom had momentarily generated a tiny current.

At last Earth was under me—the familiar Earth I knew—and I was dropping down toward the upper end of Lake Michigan. Various landmarks guided me to the little lake, inland, near which Alward's house was situated. Then I was gliding down toward the construction hangar. The *Starling* settled gently to the ground.

I was home.

IT HIT me quite suddenly. I was back at last, after all the unhappy hopeless months. And it wasn't just a dream. It was real—as real as the promise of tomorrow. As real as tears…

After a while I pulled myself together sufficiently to unbuckle my safety straps and unlock the port. As I swung to the ground, Suzanne and Alward came running from the house. The surprise and delight on their faces was a welcome more eloquent than words could ever have been.

"Charles!" Suzanne cried. "Charles—you're back! You've come back!"

"Back to stay," I said against her hair.

"Did the ship work?" Alward asked impatiently. "But why were you gone so long? It's been almost two weeks since you left. And…and where's Dan?"

My story took up most of the afternoon. I don't think Alward and Suzanne actually fully believed me until I showed them Burdeen's letter and the articles, which I had brought with me from Ard. Even then it took quite a while for them to grasp the extent of my adventure. And I was called upon for days afterward to recount various aspects and phases of it. I don't think that the wonder of it ever dulled for them. I know it will never dull for me. In my mind, memories of Ard, of Julon, and of the Omni-mech will always be shining and bright.

I should end here, but it really needs one more detail to conclude my narrative satisfactorily.

Several days later, Alward told me of a new project upon which he was working. "I never thought of the time flaw in my principle, Charles, and this because the principle itself opened up new vistas which blinded me to everything else. You see, I have come to realize that it is not an end in itself, but the means to an end. It is the basis for something bigger, more significant. The calculations I am now engaged in working out will, I feel, in time lead to a vastly superior method of interstellar travel than that which the principle first suggested. It is linked with hyperspace."

Alward looked as though he expected me to be surprised, but I'd been expecting this sooner or later. I'd said nothing to him about the Hyperspace Equations, or the method of interstellar travel through hyperspace possessed by the ancients of Julon. It hadn't been necessary. There had been more of a link between Alward's warp generator principle and the Hyperspace Equations than the Omni-mech had guessed.

The name of the man who had created the Equations and thereby the interstellar drive had been given in the instruction sheets which I had obtained and translated for Julon. The man was Professor Alward.

THE END

If you've enjoyed this book, you will not want to miss these terrific titles...

ARMCHAIR SCI-FI & HORROR DOUBLE NOVELS, $12.95 each

D-51 **A GOD NAMED SMITH** by Henry Slesar
  WORLDS OF THE IMPERIUM by Keith Laumer

D-52 **CRAIG'S BOOK** by Don Wilcox
  EDGE OF THE KNIFE by H. Beam Piper

D-53 **THE SHINING CITY** by Rena M. Vale
  THE RED PLANET by Russ Winterbotham

D-54 **THE MAN WHO LIVED TWICE** by Rog Phillips
  VALLEY OF THE CROEN by Lee Tarbell

D-55 **OPERATION DISASTER** by Milton Lesser
  LAND OF THE DAMNED by Berkeley Livingston

D-56 **CAPTIVE OF THE CENTAURIANESS** by Poul Anderson
  A PRINCESS OF MARS by Edgar Rice Burroughs

D-57 **THE NON-STATISTICAL MAN** by Raymond F. Jones
  MISSION FROM MARS by Rick Conroy

D-58 **INTRUDERS FROM THE STARS** by Ross Rocklynne
  FLIGHT OF THE STARLING by Chester S. Geier

D-59 **COSMIC SABOTEUR** by Frank M. Robinson
  LOOK TO THE STARS by Willard Hawkins

D-60 **THE MOON IS HELL!** by John W. Campbell, Jr.
  THE GREEN WORLD by Hal Clement

ARMCHAIR SCIENCE FICTION CLASSICS, $12.95 each

C-16 **THE SHAVER MYSTERY, Book Three**
  by Richard S. Shaver

C-17 **THE GIRLS FROM PLANET 5**
  by Richard Wilson

C-18 **THE FOURTH "R"**
  by George O. Smith

ARMCHAIR SCIENCE FICTION & HORROR GEMS SERIES, $12.95 each

G-5 **SCIENCE FICTION GEMS, Vol. Three**
  C. M. Kornbluth and others

G-6 **HORROR GEMS, Vol. Three**
  August Derleth and others

If you've enjoyed this book, you will not want to miss these terrific titles…

ARMCHAIR SCI-FI, FANTASY, & HORROR DOUBLE NOVELS, $12.95 each

D-1 **THE GALAXY RAIDERS** by William P. McGivern
SPACE STATION #1 by Frank Belknap Long

D-2 **THE PROGRAMMED PEOPLE** by Jack Sharkey
SLAVES OF THE CRYSTAL BRAIN by William Carter Sawtelle

D-3 **YOU'RE ALL ALONE** by Fritz Leiber
THE LIQUID MAN by Bernard C. Gilford

D-4 **CITADEL OF THE STAR LORDS** by Edmund Hamilton
VOYAGE TO ETERNITY by Milton Lesser

D-5 **IRON MEN OF VENUS** by Don Wilcox
THE MAN WITH ABSOLUTE MOTION by Noel Loomis

D-6 **WHO SOWS THE WIND…** by Rog Phillips
THE PUZZLE PLANET by Robert A. W. Lowndes

D-7 **PLANET OF DREAD** by Murray Leinster
TWICE UPON A TIME by Charles L. Fontenay

D-8 **THE TERROR OUT OF SPACE** by Dwight V. Swain
QUEST OF THE GOLDEN APE by Ivar Jorgensen and Adam Chase

D-9 **SECRET OF MARRACOTT DEEP** by Henry Slesar
PAWN OF THE BLACK FLEET by Mark Clifton.

D-10 **BEYOND THE RINGS OF SATURN** by Robert Moore Williams
A MAN OBSESSED by Alan E. Nourse

ARMCHAIR SCIENCE FICTION CLASSICS, $12.95 each

C-1 **THE GREEN MAN**
by Harold M. Sherman

C-2 **A TRACE OF MEMORY**
By Keith Laumer

C-3 **INTO PLUTONIAN DEPTHS**
by Stanton A. Coblentz

ARMCHAIR MASTERS OF SCIENCE FICTION SERIES, $16.95 each

M-1 **MASTERS OF SCIENCE FICTION, Vol. One**
Bryce Walton—"Dark of the Moon" and other tales

M-2 **MASTERS OF SCIENCE FICTION, Vol. Two**
Jerome Bixby: "One Way Street" and other tales

If you've enjoyed this book, you will not want to miss these terrific titles…

ARMCHAIR SCI-FI & HORROR DOUBLE NOVELS, $12.95 each

D-11 **PERIL OF THE STARMEN** by Kris Neville
THE STRANGE INVASION by Murray Leinster

D-12 **THE STAR LORD** by Boyd Ellanby
CAPTIVES OF THE FLAME by Samuel R. Delaney

D-13 **MEN OF THE MORNING STAR** by Edmund Hamilton
PLANET FOR PLUNDER by Hal Clement and Sam Merwin, Jr.

D-14 **ICE CITY OF THE GORGON** by Chester S. Geier and Richard Shaver
WHEN THE WORLD TOTTERED by Lester Del Rey

D-15 **WORLDS WITHOUT END** by Clifford D. Simak
THE LAVENDER VINE OF DEATH by Don Wilcox

D-16 **SHADOW ON THE MOON** by Joe Gibson
ARMAGEDDON EARTH by Geoff St. Reynard

D-17 **THE GIRL WHO LOVED DEATH** by Paul W. Fairman
SLAVE PLANET by Laurence M. Janifer

D-18 **SECOND CHANCE** by J. F. Bone
MISSION TO A DISTANT STAR by Frank Belknap Long

D-19 **THE SYNDIC** by C. M. Kornbluth
FLIGHT TO FOREVER by Poul Anderson

D-20 **SOMEWHERE I'LL FIND YOU** by Milton Lesser
THE TIME ARMADA by Fox B. Holden

ARMCHAIR SCIENCE FICTION CLASSICS, $12.95 each

C-4 **CORPUS EARTHLING**
by Louis Charbonneau

C-5 **THE TIME DISSOLVER**
by Jerry Sohl

C-6 **WEST OF THE SUN**
by Edgar Pangborn

ARMCHAIR SCIENCE FICTION & HORROR GEMS SERIES, $12.95 each

G-1 **SCIENCE FICTION GEMS, Vol. One**
Isaac Asimov and others

G-2 **HORROR GEMS, Vol. One**
Carl Jacobi and others

If you've enjoyed this book, you will not want to miss these terrific titles…

ARMCHAIR SCI-FI, FANTASY, & HORROR DOUBLE NOVELS, $12.95 each

D-21 **EMPIRE OF EVIL** by Robert Arnette
THE SIGN OF THE TIGER by Alan E. Nourse & J. A. Meyer

D-22 **OPERATION SQUARE PEG** by Frank Belknap Long
ENCHANTRESS OF VENUS by Leigh Brackett

D-23 **THE LIFE WATCH** by Lester Del Rey
CREATURES OF THE ABYSS by Murray Leinster

D-24 **LEGION OF LAZARUS** by Edmond Hamilton
STAR HUNTER by Andre Norton

D-25 **EMPIRE OF WOMEN** by John Fletcher
ONE OF OUR CITIES IS MISSING by Irving Cox

D-26 **THE WRONG SIDE OF PARADISE** by Raymond F. Jones
THE INVOLUNTARY IMMORTALS by Rog Phillips

D-27 **EARTH QUARTER** by Damon Knight
ENVOY TO NEW WORLDS by Keith Laumer

D-28 **SLAVES TO THE METAL HORDE** by Milton Lesser
HUNTERS OUT OF TIME by Joseph E. Kelleam

D-29 **RX JUPITER SAVE US** by Ward Moore
BEWARE THE USURPERS by Geoff St. Reynard

D-30 **SECRET OF THE SERPENT** by Don Wilcox
CRUSADE ACROSS THE VOID by Dwight V. Swain

ARMCHAIR SCIENCE FICTION CLASSICS, $12.95 each

C-7 **THE SHAVER MYSTERY, Book One**
by Richard S. Shaver

C-8 **THE SHAVER MYSTERY, Book Two**
by Richard S. Shaver

C-9 **MURDER IN SPACE** by David V. Reed
by David V. Reed

ARMCHAIR MASTERS OF SCIENCE FICTION SERIES, $16.95 each

M-3 **MASTERS OF SCIENCE FICTION, Vol. Three**
Robert Sheckley, "The Perfect Woman" and other tales

M-4 **MASTERS OF SCIENCE FICTION, Vol. Four**
Mack Reynolds, "Stowaway" and other tales

If you've enjoyed this book, you will not want to miss these terrific titles…

ARMCHAIR SCI-FI, FANTASY, & HORROR DOUBLE NOVELS, $12.95 each

D-41 **FULL CYCLE** by Clifford D. Simak
IT WAS THE DAY OF THE ROBOT by Frank Belknap Long

D-42 **THIS CROWDED EARTH** by Robert Bloch
REIGN OF THE TELEPUPPETS by Daniel Galouye

D-43 **THE CRISPIN AFFAIR** by Jack Sharkey
THE RED HELL OF JUPITER by Paul Ernst

D-44 **PLANET OF DREAD** by Dwight V. Swain
WE THE MACHINE by Gerald Vance

D-45 **THE STAR HUNTER** by Edmond Hamilton
THE ALIEN by Raymond F. Jones

D-46 **WORLD OF IF** by Rog Phillips
SLAVE RAIDERS FROM MERCURY by Don Wilcox

D-47 **THE ULTIMATE PERIL** by Robert Abernathy
PLANET OF SHAME by Bruce Elliot

D-48 **THE FLYING EYES** by J. Hunter Holly
SOME FABULOUS YONDER by Phillip Jose Farmer

D-49 **THE COSMIC BUNGLARS** by Geoff St. Reynard
THE BUTTONED SKY by Geoff St. Reynard

D-50 **TYRANTS OF TIME** by Milton Lesser
PARIAH PLANET by Murray Leinster

ARMCHAIR SCIENCE FICTION CLASSICS, $12.95 each

C-13 **SUNKEN WORLD**
by Stanton A. Coblentz

C-14 **THE LAST VIAL**
by Sam McClatchie, M. D.

C-15 **WE WHO SURVIVED (THE FIFTH ICE AGE)**
by Sterling Noel

ARMCHAIR MASTERS OF SCIENCE FICTION SERIES, $16.95 each

MS-5 **MASTERS OF SCIENCE FICTION, Vol. Five**
Winston K. Marks—Test Colony and other tales

MS-6 **MASTERS OF SCIENCE FICTION, Vol. Six**
Fritz Leiber—Deadly Moon and other tales